"Damned if you don't look like a heifer caught in a loading chute. You tryin' to break in, or what?"

Charity, stuck in the doggy door with her posterior greeting the stranger, wasn't amused. She dropped her head to her hands in exasperation. "I'm not breaking in. I'm the *house-sitter*."

"Taking the job a bit literally, aren't you?"

A jokester. Just what she needed. "I'm stuck."

"Yep."

She detected laughter in that single syllable and she clenched her jaw. He seemed to be *enjoying* himself. But irritating though he might be, he was all she had at the moment. She swallowed her pride. "Can you pull me out?"

"Okay." He sounded dubious.

After a short pause, he enclosed her hips in the firm vise of his arms. She realized she should be embarrassed by being in such an intimate situation with a stranger, but instead she was grateful for the blissful warmth surrounding her bottom as he hugged her close. As the man's fingers tightened on Charity's behind, the dog ventured back into the room and started licking her face.

"Cut that out," she ordered.

Her rescuer snorted. "If I may say so, ma'am, you're in no position to question my technique."

Dear Reader,

With the seasons changing and thoughts of winter not so far off, what better way to keep up our spirits than with a good dose of love and laughter?

This month we are thrilled to offer two charming and wonderful books written by two very popular authors. Vicki Lewis Thompson is a regular contributor to Harlequin Temptation and Superromance. Her light and lively style makes her a natural for writing LOVE & LAUGHTER, and her story about a pair of unlikely lovers trapped together is filled with tension and humor—and a truly wacky neighbor. I think we can all relate to the heroine's predicament: meeting an absolutely gorgeous guy while stuck in a doggy door!

Ruth Jean Dale continues to be a writing sensation. She launched her career in Temptation but then quickly branched out into Harlequin Romance, Superromance and Historical. *The Seven-Year Itch* is funny and romantic, a treat to read. Ivy's attempted revenge on her husband's *supposed* infidelity backfires in the most delightful ways....

With love—and laughter,

Malle Vallik

Malle Vallik
Associate Senior Editor

STUCK ~~ON~~ ^{With} YOU

Vicki Lewis Thompson

Harlequin Books

TORONTO • NEW YORK • LONDON
AMSTERDAM • PARIS • SYDNEY • HAMBURG
STOCKHOLM • ATHENS • TOKYO • MILAN
MADRID • WARSAW • BUDAPEST • AUCKLAND

ISBN 0-373-44005-7

STUCK WITH YOU

Copyright © 1996 by Vicki Lewis Thompson

This edition published by arrangement with Harlequin Books S.A.

® and TM are trademarks of the publisher. Trademarks indicated with
® are registered in the United States Patent and Trademark Office, the
Canadian Trade Marks Office and in other countries.

Printed in U.S.A.

Vicki Lewis Thompson has never installed a doggy door in her house because it's an odds-on bet she'd get stuck in it after locking herself out. Despite a key chain loaded with enough fobs and doodads to supply a souvenir shop, she's locked herself out of her car so often that AAA plans to institute a Golden Jimmy Bar Award in her name. The world has yet to come up with a flashing neon chain that talks, so Vicki's friends and family have learned to herald her departure with five precious little words: *Do you have your keys?*

Books by Vicki Lewis Thompson

HARLEQUIN TEMPTATION
484—LOVERBOY
502—WEDDING SONG
516—THE BOUNTY HUNTER
555—THE TRAILBLAZER
559—THE DRIFTER
563—THE LAWMAN
600—HOLDING OUT FOR A HERO

For Walt Nett and Gunther Burpus.
Thanks a million, guys.

1

CHARITY WEBSTER knelt in front of the doggy door. The bricks of Nora's back walkway sent cold straight through her wool slacks, and her knees quickly began to tingle and grow numb. She pushed one gloved hand against the magnetized flap, opening it enough to reach through and pat the polished wood floor in search of the key.

No luck.

With a sigh she pulled her hand back out, lowered her head and butted her way inside. Her view encompassed a small square of the honey pine floor, but the key wasn't anywhere in sight. Too bad she'd thrown it through the door with such enthusiasm that morning. Crawling in one hand at a time, she eased forward, angling her shoulders to work them through the narrow opening. In the process the flap dragged her green beret from her head.

As Charity wiggled through further, warm, potpourri-scented air laced with the lemon tang of floor wax caressed her face, making her chilled back end seem even colder. The key, attached to a key ring decorated with a football-shaped piece of Waterford crystal, lay almost within reach. Just a little more of a stretch and she'd have it.

With a yelp of pleasure MacDougal, Nora's little black Scottie, jumped from his wicker bed by the back door and trotted over, dog tags jingling, to lick Charity's face.

"Not now, Mac," she said. "I can't—damn." MacDougal's vociferous greeting knocked her glasses off, turning her whole world fuzzy. She groped for the glasses. Meanwhile, MacDougal, warming up to the playtime they'd shared every afternoon during the week Charity had been house-sitting, snatched her beret in his teeth and dashed into the kitchen with it.

"Mac," she called, "bring that—oh, to heck with it. Just don't chew it." She replaced her glasses and inched toward the glittering key ring. The tip of her fingers brushed the crystal just as MacDougal ran back in with the beret. In the process of skidding to a stop, he pushed the key ring out of reach.

Charity groaned. "You are *not* helping, and if I don't get that key, you won't get your dinner, fuzz-face. Nora's not coming back tonight after all."

MacDougal cocked his head. Eyes bright as polished onyx peeked at her from under shaggy eyebrows, and the green beret still dangled from his whiskered mouth.

In spite of her frustration, Charity laughed. "If only you were a St. Bernard I wouldn't be in this fix, mutt."

She was so close. She stretched until she was afraid her shoulder would dislocate. The exertion, coupled with wearing her quilted ski jacket in the heated interior, was making her sweat. It was a weird feeling, sweating on one end and freezing on the other.

She realized she'd have to squeeze through the door a little more, but her bulky jacket made that difficult. She should have taken it off before starting this maneuver, but she hated to back out and go through it all again when she was so close. The ankles of her socks were getting wet, which told her that the snow that had been threatening all day had begun to fall.

A little more. She gained an inch. There. Her fingers closed around the Waterford football.

"Got it, Mac!" She started to back out again. Nothing happened. She pushed again and realized that the waist of her ski jacket had wadded up around the inside of the opening. She pushed, she squeezed, she swore. Finally she flopped forward on the polished wood floor with a moan.

She was stuck.

WYATT LOGAN heaved his large duffel bag out of the back of the taxi, paid the cabbie and started up the walk toward his aunt Nora's two-story Colonial. Wet snow swirled under the brim of his cowboy hat and kissed his cheeks. Snow for Thanksgiving. He was suddenly very glad he was spending the brief holiday at Aunt Nora's instead of in some impersonal hotel room in New York City. Flying all the way home to Arizona just to eat turkey hadn't made much sense, but hopping a train to Old Saybrook, Connecticut, had been a breeze.

He mounted the porch steps, his boots slipping a bit on the wet wood, and clacked the brass knocker several times. While he waited he glanced around. The house was the last one on a street that dead-ended at a little cove where he'd loved to fish during summer visits with his folks. He hadn't been back since he was fifteen.

The neatly clipped front lawn was winter-brown now, but the twin fir trees on either side of the front walk rose just as majestically as he remembered them. In the side yard a giant maple, leafless and skeletal, arched over the roofs of Aunt Nora's house and her neighbor's. Long ago he'd spent hours climbing it and pretending the branches were rodeo bulls. Wyatt smiled to himself. He hadn't changed all that much in twenty years.

From inside the house came high-pitched barking, which reminded him that last Christmas his aunt had broken her pattern of total independence and adopted a dog. She'd even sent a picture of the animal out to Arizona, the way someone would send a picture of a new baby. The dog's name, MacDougal, had stuck in Wyatt's mind because Aunt Nora had mentioned that it meant "son of the dark stranger" in Scottish. MacDougal was a pound puppy with an unknown daddy, apparently. His aunt seemed to adore the dog.

Maybe she was getting lonely as she got older, just as his parents had said. For the first time Wyatt wondered if he might be as much company for her on this holiday as she was for him. It was a novel thought. His parents used to joke that beside the word *self-sufficient* in the dictionary there would be a picture of Nora Logan.

He rapped again, but he was coming to the conclusion she wasn't home. Probably ran to the market for some last-minute item for tomorrow's dinner, he thought.

Then he heard the call for help.

There it was again, coming from inside. He quickly tried the front door. Locked. Abandoning his duffel bag, he pounded down the steps and started around the side of the house toward the back door. Aunt Nora wasn't elderly by any stretch of the imagination, but he supposed she could have had some accident inside the house. He broke into a jog and nearly fell as his smooth-soled boots skidded on the wet leaves under the maple tree.

As he rounded the house, half running, half skating, he slid to a stop and nearly fell in his astonishment. MacDougal had a doggy door.

And somebody's butt was sticking out of it.

WHEN SHE HEARD the rap of the door knocker, Charity's first reaction was fear of being discovered in such an embarrassing position. Then reason, along with the prickling pain in her knees and toes, convinced her that embarrassment was preferable to frostbite. She needed help. So she revved up vocal chords not used to the unladylike behavior of yelling, and hollered. MacDougal took off at the unexpected racket.

She called out again, and strained to hear if there was any response. Were those footsteps, or her imagination?

"Damned if you don't look like a heifer caught in the loading chute," said a male voice from somewhere behind her. "You tryin' to break into this house or what?"

Charity dropped her head to her hands in exasperation. "I'm not breaking in. I'm the *house sitter.*"

"Taking the job a bit literally, aren't you?"

A jokester. Just what she needed. "I'm stuck!"

"Yep." The single word of agreement was followed by a long silence.

"You still there?"

"Yep."

She detected laughter in that single syllable and she clenched her jaw. He seemed to be *enjoying* himself. But irritating though he might be, he was all she had at the moment. She swallowed her pride. "Can you help get me out, please?" she called.

"I'm studyin' the situation."

"Can't you just pull me out?"

"You sure that's what you want?"

"Yes! Do something! My top half's roasting and my bottom half's freezing!"

"Okay." He sounded dubious.

After another pause, he enclosed her hips in the firm vise of his arms. She realized she should be embarrassed by being in such an intimate situation with a stranger, but she was grateful for the blissful warmth surrounding her bottom as he hugged her close. She tried not to think of what the scene might look like to an observer. With luck there would be no one watching. She hoped this man was a traveling encyclopedia salesman. That way, she'd never have to see him again.

As the man's fingers tightened on Charity's bottom, MacDougal ventured back into the room and started licking her face.

"Cut that out!" she ordered.

Her rescuer snorted. "If I may say so, ma'am, you're in no position to question my technique."

"Oh, for pity's sake. I meant the dog. Just get me out."

"Okay. Here goes."

Grunting with the effort, he pulled, and she heard something rip. Her treasured ski jacket. The one her brothers had saved paper route money to buy her. Irreplaceable. "Stop!" she yelled.

The tugging subsided, but the firm grip remained. "What's the matter?" He sounded out of breath.

"My jacket's ripping!"

"So get another jacket!"

"I can't! I'm sentimentally attached to this one!"

Abruptly his grip relaxed and the comforting warmth disappeared.

"Are you still there?" she called.

No answer. He'd left her. Just because she didn't want to ruin her jacket in this endeavor, he'd lost patience and left her to freeze her buns off in a Connecticut snowstorm. Chivalry was indeed dead. And she was in one hell of a predicament.

If only she hadn't been wearing this particular jacket. She would have sacrificed anything else in her closet, but for ten winters the jacket had warmed her, not only with its down lining, but with the memory of that special Christmas when her two brothers had presented it as if giving her diamonds. And diamonds wouldn't have been appreciated nearly as much.

Well, she'd just have to get herself out of this doggy door. Nora would never have allowed her fate to rest with some man who happened by, so neither would she. She'd—

Her thoughts were interrupted by something that felt like a metal plate sliding against her hip toward the doggy door casing. She was filled with foreboding.

"You're doing something, aren't you?" she called nervously.

"Just hold still."

"I demand to know what you're doing!"

"I found a hoe leaning against the garage."

"A hoe? Good Lord!" She swiveled as far as possible to look behind her, and from the corner of her eye she could see, sure enough, the green metal blade of a hoe slide through the side of the doggy door. "Take that thing out of there! You'll damage the door!"

"It's the door or your jacket, lady."

"Wait! Let's talk about—"

Whatever she'd meant to say was drowned out by the crack of thick plastic and the splinter of wood as the doggy door popped out, bringing her with it. She sat

down hard on the brick sidewalk, the cracked frame of
the doggy door still around her middle, while snowflakes pelted her face and hair.

With a joyous bark MacDougal bounded out after
her, splashed through a mud puddle and ran back to
launch himself at her. With legs so short his coat
brushed the ground, MacDougal could get filthy faster
than any dog she knew. Mud flew into her face, dot-
ting her glasses and splotching her cheeks.

"Ugh." As she held the wriggling dog, the sound of
muffled laughter filtered through her discomfort. She
glanced up as best she could through speckled lenses
that were already steaming up in the cold. Through the
speckles and the fog she managed to record cowboy
boots, snug jeans, a brown suede jacket and a cowboy
hat pulled low over a face burnished by the sun. She
couldn't see his eyes, but his wide grin revealed even
teeth as white as the pelting snow.

She deposited MacDougal on the ground. "I suppose you think this is funny."

"Sorry, but I think this is hilarious." He leaned forward, still wearing that infuriating smile, and held out
his hand. "Let me help you up."

"No, thank you." She didn't look at him, certain he
was still amusing himself at her expense, as she tot-
tered awkwardly to her feet. Once she was upright and
could smooth the jacket over her hips, the mangled
doggy door frame edged slowly down and clattered to
the brick walk. She stepped out of it with a sigh of relief. Free. But she was afraid to look at Nora's back
door.

When she finally forced herself to wipe the moisture
from her glasses and take inventory, she gasped in dismay. Pieces of the wooden door had been ripped out

and a ragged hole remained. "The whole door will have to be replaced," she moaned, turning back to him. "If you'd only waited, we might have been able to think of something else."

He glanced up at the sky. "I figured waiting was a mistake. It'll be dark soon, and before long you would have created a real interesting ice sculpture."

"I still say we could have—"

"You said you were sentimentally attached to that jacket. I don't reckon Aunt Nora's sentimentally attached to her door."

She stared at him as the last statement sunk in. *Aunt Nora,* he'd said. Nora had talked about her nephew with pride and love. "You're Wyatt Logan?"

He touched the brim of his hat. "At your service, ma'am."

Not wanting to be charmed, she was anyway. She took off her glasses and cleaned them again. "The bull rider."

"When I'm lucky, I ride 'em. Other times I just fall off and make a fool of myself."

She couldn't help smiling. "Unfortunately, Nora's not here."

"I figured that one out all by myself. It was that word *house sitter* that gave it away. By the way, who are you?"

"Charity Webster. I own a bookstore in town and I'm a friend of Nora's."

"That figures. My aunt loves books."

"She meant to be back today. Did she know you were coming?"

He nodded. "She found out I'd be in the area this week for a rodeo at the Garden. She invited me for Thanksgiving."

"Oh, dear." Charity frowned. "Well, I'm sure she'll hurry back as soon as she can. She called me at work this afternoon to say the Bangor airport is paralyzed with this storm and she wondered if I could keep feeding MacDougal for her. In all the confusion she must have forgotten you were due to arrive."

He shrugged. "No big deal, Charity. I can fend for myself."

Sympathy tugged at her. He'd come here planning to be with family for Thanksgiving, and he might end up spending the day alone. Of course, so would she, but she'd already accepted the idea, and it was for a good cause. She needed to keep the store open on Friday, so driving to Boston to see her mother wasn't practical.

"I take it you tossed the keys through the flap when you left this morning," he said.

"Right."

"That's good to know. I'd hate to think you'd been crawling in and out of the doggy door all week."

Her sympathy dimmed and she gave him a withering look. "Nora did mention that you could be a smart aleck."

He feigned dismay. "My devoted auntie said such a thing about her favorite nephew?"

"Her only nephew, if I remember correctly."

"And cherished all the more because of it," he said. "Listen, the snow's getting heavier. We'd probably better find a way to fix that door."

"You're right." Charity glanced at the gaping hole in despair. Snow was already swirling through it. "But I have no idea how. We certainly couldn't get a new door at this late date." She polished her glasses again and glanced at her watch. "The hardware store closes in ten minutes."

"Are the keys to Nora's Mercedes on that ring you worked so hard to get?"

She glanced at the ring in her hand. "Yes, but—"

"Why don't you unlock the door, then give them to me? I'll make a run to the hardware store."

She hesitated.

"Unless you want to just give me the keys and crawl through the hole in the door. You should fit now."

She let out a sigh of exasperation. Nora had urged her to use the car, but her bookstore wasn't far away and she'd chosen to walk instead of taking the expensive car out of the garage. "It's just that I feel responsible for everything around here. I'd hate to have anything happen to the Mercedes."

"Are you implying I can't drive it?"

"No. I just—"

"Because you can drive there, if you want. We can't both go, with this hole in the door. We're down to seven minutes, now."

"I wouldn't know what to buy. I'm no carpenter." She gazed at him. "Will you promise to be careful?"

"I'm always careful. Six-and-a-half minutes and counting."

"I guess there's not much choice." Charity walked over and unlocked the door before handing him the key ring.

He moved quickly toward the side door of the garage, which he unlocked in no time. Then he turned. "Would you bring my duffel bag in from the front porch? I left it there when I heard you calling."

"Sure."

"By the way, how do I get to the hardware store?"

She'd assumed he knew his way around, but apparently he didn't. Her misgivings grew, but she still couldn't see any alternative, so she gave him directions. As he disappeared into the garage, Charity thought of something else. Wyatt was from southern Arizona, where it hardly ever snowed. She hurried over to the door and peered in just as he pushed the automatic garage door opener and hopped into the car.

"Wait! Have you ever driven in these conditions?" she called into the gloom.

He started the engine and buzzed the automatic window down before answering. "Compared to riding a bull, how hard can it be?" With a cocky smile of farewell, he backed out of the garage much too fast. The car's back end fishtailed, barely missing Nora's mailbox as Wyatt swerved the car into the street.

Charity closed her eyes and leaned her head against the doorjamb. "My life is over," she muttered.

"Well, now, this is a bit of a sticky wicket," commented a man from somewhere behind her.

Charity's shoulders sagged. The last person she wanted to deal with at the moment was Nora's prissy neighbor, Alistair Updegraff. In addition to being Nora's only neighbor on the rural side street, he was Charity's best customer at the bookstore. A retired schoolteacher who had been widowed five years ago, he gobbled up mysteries at the rate of several a week, and he wasn't averse to buying hardbound copies, either. Without him, her slim profit margin would be in trouble.

So she took a deep breath and turned with the most pleasant expression she could muster. "Hello, Mr. Updegraff. Yes, I'm afraid we've had a little problem here this afternoon."

"Nora's not going to be happy about that door." Built round and low to the ground, Alistair reminded

Charity of a peg person from a Fisher-Price playset. A peg person with no fashion sense. This afternoon he was decked out in a red buffalo-plaid jacket, yellow earmuffs and a purple knit cap with a Day-Glo-orange pom-pom on top.

"I'm not happy about it, either, Mr. Updegraff." Charity started to edge away. "In fact, I need to go inside and find something to put over the hole before more snow blows in."

"How'd it happen?" Alistair sidled in the same direction.

"I got stuck in the doggy door." She backed toward the house. "Long story."

"I saw somebody drive away in Nora's Mercedes. Didn't look like Nora."

"No, it was her nephew from Arizona, gone to get materials to put a temporary patch on the door. He'll take over the house-sitting now, I imagine."

"Take over?" Alistair followed her toward the doorway, his orange pom-pom bobbing. "But Nora's due back today. In fact, she should be here by now."

"True." Charity was amazed at how closely Alistair kept track of Nora's schedule. He really had a bad case for her. She reached behind her for the doorknob. "But the storm has stranded her in Maine for the time being."

"Really? That's unfortunate. And her nephew is here to visit?"

"Yes." Charity mentally turned Alistair over to Wyatt. The nosy neighbor came with the house. Wyatt would find that out, just as she had. She'd warn Wyatt to be polite. Nora believed that a woman living alone couldn't afford to antagonize her only neighbor, no matter how irritating he might be. "Now I must go in

and find something for this door. Come, Mac-
Dougal."

"I might have something. In fact, I'm sure that I—"

"Thank you, but I know just the thing," Charity said
as she opened the door. She had no idea what she'd use
to block the hole until Wyatt returned, but if she let
Alistair get into the act, he'd be entrenched for the evening. "See you later, Mr. Updegraff. Stay warm, now."
She slipped inside with MacDougal, grabbed the dog's
collar so he wouldn't run all over the house in his
muddy condition, and shut the door firmly.

Alistair leaned down and peered through the hole.
"I'll come over later and see how you made out," he
promised.

"Thanks, but that won't be necessary." Solid doors
were designed to protect against people like Alistair, she
decided. "Everything will be fine." Scooping Mac-
Dougal into her arms, she headed for the laundry room.

When she'd cleaned most of the mud off Mac-
Dougal and herself with an old towel, she moved cautiously back into the kitchen and peered out the
window. No sign of Alistair, but a puddle of melted
snow lay on the pine floor in front of the hole in the
door. "Maybe he crawled in and melted, just like the
Wicked Witch of the West," she said to MacDougal.

The Scottie woofed a response.

"Yeah, well, that wouldn't be so good for business,
I guess." She rummaged in a kitchen cabinet and came
up with heavy-duty aluminum foil designed for barbe-
cuing and a roll of masking tape. In a few minutes she'd
covered the hole well enough to stop the snow. After
wiping up the water, she went through the house turning on lights against the encroaching darkness.

In the process she noticed the message light blinking on Nora's answering machine. She'd been instructed to take messages off the machine and answer any critical ones, so she pushed the Play button.

Nora's voice came on. Charity noticed there was the same vibrant note of excitement in her tone this time as there had been when she'd called earlier in the afternoon, almost as if she were holding fast to a wonderful secret.

"Hi, Charity. If you're listening to this then you've successfully retrieved the key and are back in the house. I just remembered that my nephew and godson, Wyatt, is due to arrive anytime. He's expecting Auntie Nora to cook him Thanksgiving dinner, poor boy. I feel just awful about inviting him to an empty house and a cold stove. I realize this is a dreadful imposition, but it would mean the world to me if you'd stay on in the house and cook him that dinner. I know the turkey's thawing in the refrigerator because I asked you to put it there. Don't bother to go back home for your things. We wear the same size, so feel free to borrow anything in the closet."

Charity stared at the machine. Stay and play hostess for this cheeky bull rider? Not likely!

"Besides giving Wyatt a little company," the message continued, "you might also protect my antiques from annihilation. Wyatt's a dear boy but he comes from the wild and woolly West and tends to be a bit reckless."

The noose of obligation tightened around Charity. She grimaced as she glanced back at the kitchen door and thought about Wyatt driving around in Nora's classic Mercedes. The warning might have come just a tad too late, Nora, she thought.

"Wyatt, if you're listening, too," Nora continued, "this isn't anything I haven't said to your face. So convince Charity to stay and cook that dinner for both of you, and have a good time without me. There's a sensational merlot in the wine rack. Just make sure Mac doesn't get any. I'll be home as soon as I can. 'Bye.''

Charity swore quietly to herself as she rewound the tape. After all Nora had done for her, she would be an ungrateful wretch to deny the first real favor Nora asked. House-sitting didn't count. She'd loved staying here. A favor was something you didn't want to do, like staying on and cooking Thanksgiving dinner for Wyatt Logan, bull rider. But if that was what Nora wanted, that's what Charity would do.

2

On the return trip to Nora's house, snow flying at him through the beam of the car's headlights, Wyatt had more respect for the slippery streets and the officers of the law patrolling them. Somehow he'd talked the cop out of giving him a ticket on his way to the hardware store, but then the store had been locked up tight. Fortunately the owner hadn't left yet and Wyatt had roused him from the back with some hefty knocking. This visit to Saybrook wasn't turning out to be the sort of holiday he'd envisioned.

But it had been a hell of a lot of fun so far.

Wyatt chuckled every time he thought about Charity's fanny sticking out of the doggy door. The picture had become even funnier when he'd gotten a look at the front half of her and realized from the prim topknot of blond hair, the oversize glasses and tiny gold earrings, that she was not the sort who usually landed herself in such a fix.

Then MacDougal had put the final touch on the scene with a generous spray of mud. Wyatt had tried to control himself in consideration of Charity's feelings. He could tell that she didn't think any of it was particularly funny, but it had been very tough not to laugh.

To think he'd been worried that he might be bored spending the holiday with Aunt Nora. Of course, once

Charity left, things could get a bit dull. Not that she was his type. He stayed away from intellectual women, and if she owned a bookstore, she probably qualified. But intellectual or not, when he'd held her close to pull her from the door, she'd felt very. . . nice.

If he was brutally honest with himself, he'd squeezed the part Charity had presented to him and fantasized about the rest of her—waves of lustrous hair curling around her shoulders, bedroom eyes, pouting lips and generous breasts. His type. So much for fantasy.

He pulled into the driveway and activated the garage door opener he'd found in the glove compartment. He then unloaded the piece of plywood, taking it through the side door into the backyard and propping it against the house. His presence caused MacDougal to start yipping, and Charity peeked out the kitchen window. He raised a hand in greeting and she waved back, a smile of welcome on her face.

Or, more likely, it was a smile of relief, he thought. She'd been sure he'd wrap the Mercedes around a telephone pole. He wouldn't tell her how close he'd come to doing just that. He noticed that she'd used aluminum foil as a temporary repair for the door and gave her points for ingenuity.

Lights were on and the house beckoned as a warm haven from the snowy night. At times like these Wyatt understood why men gave up the single life in favor of a cozy home and a steadfast woman. But those comforts came with a price. As it was, Wyatt didn't have to consider how his risky profession would affect someone else, and that was the way he liked it.

He found the tools he'd need in the garage—a hand saw, a screwdriver and a cordless drill. Taking them, along with the bag of nuts and screws he'd bought, he headed for the back door of the house.

Charity opened it for him. MacDougal sat beside her like a good little soldier. He'd obviously been commanded to sit, but his rear end wiggled in greeting.

"So you made it," she said.

"Never had any doubt."

"The car's okay?"

"Perfect." He started to put the tools on a small table by the back door.

"Not there!" Charity rushed forward, and Mac-Dougal grabbed the chance to break his sit and run forward, too. "That's a Hepplewhite."

He paused, frowning. "Which means?"

"An antique. It's priceless."

He snorted. "Then God knows why she set it by the back door where people are bound to put stuff. Do you understand that, MacDougal?"

The little dog woofed once.

"I didn't think so." Wyatt started to deposit the tools and the bag of screws on the floor, then paused. "Is this okay, or is the floor a Frank Lloyd Wright or something?"

"You do have a smart mouth. Of course the floor's okay. We walk on it."

"That's a relief." After he laid down his supplies MacDougal hurried over to sniff everything. Wyatt gave him a pat before straightening and glancing at Charity.

She'd taken off the ski jacket that had been responsible for the whole episode and washed her face and glasses free of mud. He took in the high-collared white blouse, buttoned to her throat, the repinned topknot and the round-framed glasses. Behind them her eyes were an intelligent blue that seemed to be assessing him,

as well. Her cheeks looked pink and soft as a baby's receiving blanket and her skin had the sort of flawless
perfection that required no makeup. She wore no lipstick, which left her mouth a vulnerable shade of pale
rose.

He had the inane thought that a woman who didn't
wear lipstick would always be ready to be kissed. The
thought was inane because everything about Charity
Webster was the opposite of his usual choice in female
companionship. Besides, it was past time for her to
leave and get on with her own activities. For all he knew
she had a date for tonight and he was holding her up.

"I can take it from here," he said. "I'm sure you
have things to do. And don't worry about the door.
When Aunt Nora gets back, I'll explain that it was all
my fault that it got so torn up." He started unbut-
toning his suede jacket.

"Um, there was a message from Nora on the machine."

He looked up and noticed the pink in her cheeks had
deepened. "What did she have to say?" he prompted
when she seemed hesitant to continue.

"She, um, would like me to stay on until she gets
back."

He rested his fingers against a leather-covered button as he gazed at her. "Stay on? Why?"

"She feels terrible about leaving you on your own for
Thanksgiving, after inviting you up here. There's a turkey thawing in the refrigerator, and she asked if I'd—"

"Hey." He kept his voice gentle, still not sure what
he was dealing with. "I'm sure you have plans for
Thanksgiving, and I'm a big boy. I'm really surprised
that my aunt would impose on you that way. It isn't like
her to put people out."

Charity immediately leapt to Nora's defense. "She already knows I was staying in Saybrook for Thanksgiving, because I have to open the bookstore on Friday, and my mother lives clear up in Boston. It's not worth braving the holiday crowds to go up. She probably thought she was doing us both a favor."

That was exactly what he'd been afraid of from the moment Charity started this conversation. The next question was difficult, but he needed the answer. "Do you, uh, that is, are you involved with someone?"

Her cheeks flamed. "What in hell does that have to do with the price of beans?" She waved aside his attempt to answer. "Never mind. I can figure it out. You have some ego, Mr. Logan, if you think that I'd take one look at you and fall in with some matchmaking scheme cooked up by Nora."

"You don't understand." He hadn't figured she'd be so quick on the uptake. "Lately my parents and Nora have been—"

"I don't care if they've been parading eligible females in front of you at the rate of one a week! I'm not now, nor will I ever be, in the market for a husband!"

MacDougal whined and wriggled between them as if to silence the conflict.

"You're gay?" Wyatt asked.

She threw up her hands. "That is so *typical*. Men always assume the only reason a woman would refuse to shackle herself to a man is because of her sexual preference. Did it ever occur to you that I might value my freedom as much as a swinging bachelor such as yourself does?"

"I—"

"Of course it didn't! You see a single female and immediately classify her as a man-hungry predator who

will do anything to snag a mate. If I didn't owe Nora so
damned much, I'd walk out of this house and let you
spend your miserable Thanksgiving all by yourself. It
would serve you right."

His jaw clenched. "Then why don't you?"

"Because Nora seemed a little concerned about leaving a rough-and-tumble character like you alone among
her antiques," she said with a note of triumph. "And
after being around you for less than an hour, I understand her concern."

"Oh, is that right?" His vow to be polite evaporated. "Just name one thing I've broken."

She glanced pointedly at the door.

"That was your fault!"

She arched an eyebrow in that maddening way some
women had of looking superior. "You just said a few
moments ago that you'd claim full responsibility when
Nora came home."

He stepped forward and pushed his face closer to
hers. "I offered to take the blame because I was trying
to be a *gentleman*."

She didn't flinch. "I can see that's a difficult role for
you."

"So help me—"

"Yes?"

There was that calm air of superiority again. It challenged something male and primitive in him, something he wasn't particularly proud of, but an emotion
that had him securely in its clutches right now. He
wondered how long it had been since she'd been with a
man who could make her cry out with desire. He fought
the urge to strip away that oh-so-civilized manner of
hers to find out what the woman underneath had to say.

He won the fight and started rebuttoning his coat. "I'll fix the door, and then I'll catch a cab back to the train station. I'm sure you'd rather spend Thanksgiving here alone than with me, a member of that lowly species called man, hanging around."

"Oh. Oh, dear."

He glanced into her eyes and was surprised to see genuine distress there. "Isn't that what you want?"

"Well . . . no."

"Couldn't prove it by the way you were acting."

"The thing is . . ." She looked genuinely miserable.

"The thing is, you hate men."

"No! I don't hate men. And I think Nora will be very unhappy if she comes back and discovers I drove you away."

"She won't. I'll tell her that one of my rodeo buddies called from New York and wanted to get together. I won't blame it on you."

"Oh, please, don't be *nice.*"

He produced his most condescending smile. "And spoil my image?"

She took a deep breath. The action brought his attention to a fact he hadn't noticed before. She had lovely breasts. Too bad God had given them to a woman like Charity, who probably didn't care whether a man would find pleasure there or not.

"Look," she said, sounding very uncomfortable. "I'm sorry. Could we start over? Neither of us has any particular place to go for the holiday, and it would be a shame to let that turkey go to waste."

"Now that's a Yankee talking, if I ever heard one."

Rebellion flashed in her blue eyes, but she seemed to make a conscious effort to stamp it out. "Maybe that's part of it. The other part is that your aunt is the kindest, most generous woman I know. Without her, I wouldn't even have a bookstore to open on Friday. I'm not certain what her motives might be for suggesting we celebrate Thanksgiving together, but she's such a feminist, I can't believe it's some sort of elaborate plot to throw us into each other's arms."

"Don't bet on it."

She lifted her chin. "And even if it is, so what? Neither of us is interested in that sort of arrangement, so it won't do any harm to accede to her wishes."

Accede to her wishes. She was definitely brainy, which meant he didn't have to worry about being romantically ensnared. In his experience, brainy women made a guy work too hard in the relationship, and that wasn't his cup of tea.

"Tell you what," he said. "Let's fix the door, and if we're still speaking to each other after that, we'll give it a try. We're only talking about twenty-four hours, anyway."

"That's what I estimate."

"Then it's a deal?"

"Yes. Thanks." She let out her breath, which made her breasts quiver beneath the silky white blouse.

Wyatt told himself to ignore things like that. As a point of honor, he couldn't succumb to temptation with this woman. He felt certain that if he did, he'd be falling in with Nora's scheme. Because he believed she had one. The storm might have been a happy accident, but Nora had planned to introduce him to Charity Webster, and he only knew one reason why his aunt would do such a thing. Just like his parents, she wanted him to find a nice girl and settle down. For some unknown reason, she'd imagined Charity was the sort he'd find to his liking. Which showed how much his Aunt Nora knew.

As WYATT WENT OUTSIDE to get the plywood, Charity tried to regain some measure of poise. She couldn't remember the last time she'd felt so unsettled, and it was all Nora's fault. Well, the weather was part of it, too, but Charity couldn't quell the suspicion that from the beginning, Nora had intended to introduce her to Wyatt while he was in Saybrook for the holiday.

For one thing, just before Nora had left for Maine, she'd casually mentioned that Charity was welcome to have Thanksgiving dinner at her house, yet she'd made no mention that her nephew would be there. An oversight? Charity didn't think so. You didn't plan a meal with two guests and forget about one of them.

Charity couldn't imagine why Nora would think such a meeting was a good idea. Even if Charity was looking for a man, which she wasn't, Wyatt was the exact opposite of the type of man she'd seek. She'd look for a shy, intellectual man, not some boisterous cowboy who rode bulls. The very thought made her shudder.

Maybe Nora thought she'd be drawn in by Wyatt's looks, which were okay, if you liked that square-jawed, outdoorsy type with shoulders that filled a doorway and hands big enough to span your waist. And if you had a weakness for brown eyes, Charity admitted, his eyes might seem very attractive. When they weren't dark with anger, they warmed to the color of caramel.

But none of that made any difference to Charity. No difference whatsoever.

He came through the door with the plywood, a piece about four feet square, way too big for the hole in the door. "I'll have to cut it down," he said.

Charity pictured clouds of sawdust billowing over Nora's elegant antiques and flinched. But she couldn't make him cut the wood outside, and the garage was nearly as cold. "The laundry room," she said in sudden inspiration. "You can brace it over the washer and dryer."

"Good idea." He carried the plywood through the kitchen into the laundry room and rested it on top of the washer and dryer. On the way back into the kitchen to retrieve the saw, he shucked his jacket and hung it over the back of a chair. His Western-cut shirt was midnight black and trimmed with silver lightning bolts. He left his hat on.

"Don't you want to measure first?" Charity asked.

He pushed his hat back with his thumb. "I've already eyeballed it."

"I think the wood's going to slip on that surface when you start sawing."

He gazed at her with those caramel eyes. "I thought you didn't know anything about carpentering?"

"I don't. It's just logical."

"Are you offering to help hold it, then?"

"I guess I am."

"Well, come on. We don't have all day."

Wyatt was right-handed, so he went in first. Charity followed and stood to the right of him. The wood extended out over the tops of both the washer and dryer by nearly two feet, which made it a very tight fit for both of them and the wood in the tiny room. When MacDougal squeezed in, too, maneuvering became impossible.

"We'll have to put him out," Wyatt said.

"You're right." Charity took MacDougal by the collar and led him back into the kitchen. "You stay here," she ordered.

The Scottie looked very disappointed, but he sat, facing the laundry room door to wait.

"Good dog." Charity went back in the laundry room and closed the door after her.

"I figure about two-and-a-half feet by three feet should do it." Wyatt positioned the saw. "If you'll steady it on the dryer, I'll cut right through here, where there's a space between the two machines."

"I still think you should measure."

He paused and glanced at her, his face very close. "Do you want to do this, instead, Charity?" he asked softly.

For some silly reason her heart started beating faster as she looked into his eyes. "No," she said quickly. The room suddenly seemed much smaller.

"It must be tough for you to let a man be in control of something."

Her gaze drifted to the curve of his lower lip. "That's not it. I—"

"I think that's exactly it. But don't worry. Once the door's fixed, you can call the shots. I don't have half the macho hangups you imagine I do."

She swallowed and looked back into his eyes. Oh, God. There was sexual awareness there, and amusement. He was flirting with her. With a man like Wyatt, flirting was probably a reflex, but no one had flirted with her in a long time. She was more vulnerable than she'd realized. "Let's get this done," she said in a strangled tone. "Before the storm gets any worse."

"You're right." He turned his attention to the saw and rasped the blade back and forth several times across the edge of the wood to create a groove. Then he settled in with long, sure strokes that bit through the wood, his arm and shoulder muscles flexing rhythmically.

As Charity braced the wood against her hips, vibrations from the saw's motion set off a pleasant but disconcerting sensual response deep within her. Under different circumstances she couldn't imagine reacting this way, but she'd already felt this man's arms around a very sensitive part of her anatomy. Then there had been all that talk about Nora's intentions in bringing them together, followed by Wyatt's knowing glance and the intimacy of this little laundry room.

The sawing stopped.

"Charity?"

She took a deep breath and tried to get control of herself before she looked at him.

"Are you all right? Is the sawdust getting to you?"

"No." She closed her eyes and tried to blot out the image of satisfying her sudden, and quite embarrassing, craving.

"Something is wrong." He gripped her by her upper arms and turned her to face him. "You're all flushed."

"No!" Quickly she opened her eyes and tried to pull away. "Fair-skinned people just naturally—"

"Do they, Charity?" He held her fast and looked deep into her eyes.

She knew he'd guessed her secret when a slow smile spread across his lips. He pulled her nearer, and her heart thundered in her ears.

A steady pounding from the back door made him pause.

"Hello-o!" Alistair called. "Anybody home?"

"Who's that?" Wyatt whispered, looking annoyed.

"The neighbor," Charity whispered back. "And he knows somebody has to be here. He's probably heard the sawing and he can look through the window and see MacDougal stationed by the laundry room door. If we don't go out, no telling what he'll think."

"Ask me if I care."

"I care. He's a good customer at the bookstore and Nora wants to stay on his good side, too, living alone like she does."

Wyatt sighed and released her. "Then let's go out and meet this wonderful neighbor."

"Make sure MacDougal doesn't get in here," Charity said. "Or he'll track sawdust all over the house."

"Okay."

Charity went out first. "Coming, Mr. Updegraff," she called, walking over to the door. As she opened it to let Alistair in, Wyatt emerged from the laundry room and grabbed MacDougal's collar before he had a chance to dash inside. Then Wyatt shut the door firmly in the dog's face.

Alistair stood dripping on the floor. "What was that strange noise I heard coming from in there?" He angled his head toward the laundry room.

"Sawing. We're cutting a piece of plywood to patch the hole," Charity replied. "I'd like you to meet Nora's nephew, Wyatt Logan. Wyatt, this is Alistair Updegraff, who lives in the house next door."

"Glad to meet you, Mr. Updegraff." Wyatt stepped forward and offered his hand to the little man.

"Nora's nephew, huh?" Alistair looked Wyatt up and down as they shook hands. "From what I hear, you're the end of the line."

"I beg your pardon?"

"Heirs. Nora doesn't have any except you."

Wyatt laughed. "I suppose that's true, if she should decide to leave me anything. As you know, she's a great one for causes, especially women's causes, so they might get it all. I really don't care."

"You don't, huh?" Alistair sounded as if he didn't believe a word of it. Then he turned his attention to Charity. "Surprised to see you here. I thought the nephew was supposed to take over."

Charity groaned to herself. But she might as well tell him. He'd find out eventually, considering how closely he watched Nora's house. "Well, Nora called and suggested Wyatt and I might want to have Thanksgiving together, since she won't be able to make it. So I'll be staying on a little longer."

"Is that so?" Alistair looked from her to Wyatt. "You two know each other from before, then?"

"We'd never met before today," Wyatt said.

Charity almost laughed. The truth, stated so baldly, sounded like a cover-up. Or maybe she was just thinking the way Alistair would. "It's true," she said. "But Nora knew we'd both be alone for Thanksgiving, and she has the turkey thawing in the refrigerator, so—" Charity stopped babbling when she realized the polite gesture would be to invite Alistair, who might also be alone tomorrow. She just couldn't do it.

Alistair glanced back at the laundry room. Charity could imagine what he thought she and Wyatt had been doing in there with the door closed. She wondered if sawing wood might possibly sound like something creaking back and forth if you were—oh, dear. She felt the blush creeping up her neck.

"Was there something we could help you with, Mr. Updegraff?" she asked, desperate to get him out of the house.

"Yes. I was trying to remember the name of that bed and breakfast in Maine where Nora is staying. She's spoken so highly of it that I thought I might call and make a reservation for the spring. Wasn't it The Latchkey, or something like that?"

"That's right." Charity didn't for a minute think Alistair wanted the information so he could make a reservation. He would call tonight to tattle about the doggy door. And perhaps ask if Nora realized that Wyatt and Charity were living in sin while she was gone. Charity decided to let him do his darnedest. She'd tried her best to keep everything nice for Nora and that would have to be good enough.

"Was there anything else?" she asked. She didn't dare suggest he take off his coat, or he'd never leave.

"Well, I guess this doesn't matter, now that you're planning to stay here and all," he said, "but the highway patrol's shutting down all the roads and the trains aren't running. This storm has paralyzed the state. Everyone's advised to stay inside and keep warm."

"In that case, you'd better get back to your house," Wyatt said. "Thanks for your concern, but we're fine here."

"Need any help with that sawing?" Alistair asked, moving as if to take off the muffler wrapped around his neck.

"We're handling it," Charity said. "But thanks."

"Okay, then. Holler if you need anything." At last he left.

Charity closed the door after him and turned toward Wyatt. She'd never thought she'd thank Alistair for anything, but he'd just prevented her from making a total fool of herself with Wyatt in the laundry room. "Let's finish the repair," she said briskly.

Wyatt nodded, as if he understood the mood had changed and the opportunity for intimacy had disappeared. "Well, that settles one thing," he said.

"What's that?"

"Looks like whether you like it or not, you're stuck with me until the weather changes."

3

ALISTAIR UPDEGRAFF unlocked his back door, hurried inside and secured the dead bolt. Some folks in Old Saybrook might leave their doors unlocked, but Alistair didn't believe in such carelessness, not even for a quick trip to the neighbor's house. He wiped his feet on the welcome mat by the door.

And speaking of carelessness, Nora would be furious when she found out about that door, Alistair thought with some satisfaction as he wrenched off his knit cap and unwound the muffler from his neck. She might just disinherit that flashy nephew of hers and think twice about putting her faith in Charity Webster. Served Nora right, entrusting her house and dog to Charity when Alistair would have been more than happy to take care of things while Nora was away. More than happy.

He reached for the pulley clothesline that ran from the back door down the hall to the living room and pinned his damp hat and muffler to it. Then he took off his jacket and attached that to the line before reeling it to a red nail polish mark that indicated the garments were directly positioned over the living room radiator.

As he leaned on the kitchen counter to pull off his boots, Alistair wondered what Charity and the nephew might get up to, left alone in the house like that. Alistair didn't believe for a minute that it had been Nora's idea for Charity to stay on to cook Thanksgiving dinner for an unattached young male. No, sir. The cat was away and the mice would play. Well, they hadn't figured on Alistair Updegraff. He lined his boots precisely by the back door and headed down the hall toward the living room, his socks slipping a bit on the plastic runner. Nora was going to hear about this.

Alistair's two grown sons referred to the area around his BarcaLounger recliner as Command Central. An automatic control attached to the gold Naugahyde-covered chair motored the seat up and down. Beside the recliner sat a card table that held a cordless telephone, a master remote for the entertainment center, two sets of drugstore reading glasses, a weather-band radio, a loose-leaf notebook cataloging recorded videos of "Murder She Wrote," another loose-leaf notebook labeled Sleuthing Tips, a stack of mystery novels, and his latest purchase—a Mrs. Tea automatic tea-maker.

Alistair settled in the recliner, buzzed it to the slight tilt he preferred for phoning, and picked up the receiver to dial Information.

Five minutes later he buzzed the chair upright so fast he nearly popped out of it. He caught himself and sat very still, eyes narrowed as he tried to make sense of what he'd learned. According to the reservation clerk at The Latchkey Bed and Breakfast, Nora Logan had checked out two days ago.

Struggling to remain calm, Alistair carefully arranged the facts and tried to reason the way Jessica Fletcher did while solving a mystery on "Murder She Wrote." Fact: Nora's whereabouts were unknown. Fact: Charity Webster and Nora's nephew were in possession of Nora's house and all her belongings. Fact: Charity and the nephew had acted guilty about something when they'd come out of the laundry room. Fact: The nephew stood to inherit a small fortune from Nora.

The inescapable conclusion filled Alistair with horror. Those two had conspired to murder poor Nora and dispose of her body! That lovely lady. He felt sick to his stomach. Killed for her fortune. A classic situation. He'd read it hundreds of times, and now here it was in real life. Terrible, just terrible. Not to mention what such a scandal might do to property values.

Finally he gained control of himself enough to pick up the phone and call the police. Then he replaced the receiver without dialing. He had no proof, no proof at all. Jessica Fletcher would build an airtight case before she made an accusation like that. Alistair straightened his spine as he realized the challenge thrust upon him. Having a job to do made him feel infinitely better. He must gather evidence against this evil pair and then expose them as scheming, cold-blooded killers. They were clever, but he would be more clever. He picked up the notebook labeled Sleuthing Tips. Tonight he would plan.

CHARITY CLOSED MacDougal in the downstairs powder room so that she could leave the laundry room door open while she and Wyatt finished sawing the plywood patch for the door. MacDougal whined at first but finally settled down. Charity hated to barricade the little dog away, but it was preferable to closing herself in with Wyatt again.

She didn't want to take any more chances that this virile cowboy would get the wrong idea. He looked like the type who would grab his fun where he could find it. Charity didn't relish being the holiday entertainment for a love 'em and leave 'em rodeo bum, and besides, she couldn't imagine facing Nora again after becoming the latest notch on Wyatt's custom-tooled belt.

With the laundry room door open, the last of the sawing proceeded without incident. Charity went to get the broom and dustpan from the pantry while Wyatt carried the piece of wood back out to the kitchen.

"Don't sweep yet," Wyatt said as he propped the wood against a cabinet door and turned to find her with the broom in her hand. "After I put the patch on the door I'm going to cut up the scraps for kindling."

With every comment he made she understood more fully why Nora didn't dare leave him alone in this house. "There's no reason for kindling. Nora doesn't ever use her fireplace," she said.

"You're kidding."

"No. She's never burned anything in it."

Wyatt stared at her as if she were speaking Swahili. "Do you mean to tell me that I'm in Connecticut the night before Thanksgiving, in the middle of a snowstorm, in a Colonial-style house with a big fireplace, and we're not going to use it?"

Charity had to admit a cozy fire sounded nice with the wind howling outside and snow pelting the windows, but she'd no more light a fire in Nora's imported-marble fireplace than she'd seduce Alistair Updegraff. "It's designed to be decorative and Nora doesn't want it scorched."

"Really."

She reacted to the censure in his voice with a flash of loyalty for Nora's decision. "Everybody knows an open fire is an inefficient method of heating and would only dry out the wood of Nora's antiques. The electric furnace and built-in humidifier are brand-new and perfectly adequate."

"That's not the point." Wyatt gazed at her. "An electric furnace has zero charm. Nobody's ever taken a cup of hot chocolate to go sit in front of a furnace."

She looked into his fawn-colored eyes and came up with a vivid picture of sharing hot chocolate with Wyatt in front of a roaring fire. It wasn't much of a leap to imagine a passionate, cocoa-flavored kiss as Wyatt pulled her down to the soft nap of the antique Sultanabad rug. She forced her glance away from his. "The point is that we're in someone else's house, and we will respect her wishes concerning it."

Wyatt sighed and shook his head. "I never realized Aunt Nora was so uptight about her possessions."

Her glance swung back to his. "She most certainly is *not* uptight." She planted the broom like a standard beside her. "There's nothing wrong with wanting to preserve the things you've worked a lifetime to collect."

"You look like Joan of Arc about to march into battle," he said, amusement in his gaze. "Don't get me wrong. I love my aunt and I don't want to ruin anything she sets great store by. I've never understood how people can get so attached to sticks of furniture, and a fireplace that you can't burn makes no sense to me, but..." He shrugged. "I can live with it."

His admission that he loved his aunt prompted Charity to reveal her private theory about Nora's fireplace, a theory she'd never mentioned to anyone. "I think it's more than her concern for antiques. I think she might be afraid of fire after what happened to your grandparents."

Wyatt seemed to think that over. "I guess it's possible, but my dad doesn't seem the least bit nervous about fire, and they were his parents, too. We have a huge stone fireplace at the ranch and we use it whenever the temperature goes below fifty outside."

"People don't always react the same to trauma. Did you know she has a sprinkler system in her bedroom?"

"She does? Guess I never noticed. And I was only here in the summer as a kid, so the subject of using the fireplace never came up." Wyatt rubbed his jaw. "Well, if she's afraid she might die in a house fire, why bother putting in a fireplace?"

"I don't know," Charity admitted. "Tradition, maybe. It goes with the antiques."

"Hmm. Well, it doesn't matter, anyway. We just won't build a fire."

"Right. I'll go clean the laundry room." She headed in that direction.

She should have felt relieved that they'd settled the matter, but instead the romantic image of a crackling fire haunted her as she swept up the sawdust. It would have been the perfect thing for a night like this, she thought with regret. Dangerous to her heart, perhaps, considering Wyatt's appeal, but perfect nevertheless. She'd often wished her own little duplex had a fireplace. And come to think of it, a fireplace that was never meant to be used was a waste of money and materials. She wouldn't admit to Wyatt that she agreed with him on that point, however. Give him an inch and he'd take . . . more than she was willing to give.

By the time she'd finished sweeping and returned to the kitchen, Wyatt had drilled four holes in the plywood. She decided to leave MacDougal penned up until the job was finished.

Wyatt crouched by the door and held the plywood up to the damaged portion.

Because Charity knew he wouldn't be able to see her, she watched the flex of his muscles beneath the soft fabric of his shirt and admired the shape of his broad back that narrowed to slim hips. His position forced the belted waistband of his jeans slightly away from the small of his back and pulled the denim tight across his buttocks. She'd always imagined herself attracted to a man's mind rather than his physique. She'd imagined wrong. Wyatt's mind was totally irrelevant at the moment.

"If you're finished gawking, I could use some help holding this up to the door so I can mark where to drill the holes," Wyatt said over his shoulder.

"I was not gawking!" Heat flooded her cheeks. "And anyway, how would you know what I was doing?"

"You were so quiet I checked your reflection in the window to make sure you weren't sneaking up on me with an upraised knife."

"Oh, for pity's sake!" She glanced across at the window over the kitchen sink and, sure enough, she was reflected against the darkened, frosty glass. "Besides, I wasn't looking at you. I was . . . thinking," she muttered.

His answering chuckle sizzled along her nerve endings. "Bring a pencil, and mark these holes, please, Charity."

She pulled out a drawer where Nora kept odds and ends and found a stubby pencil. Then she walked over and crouched next to Wyatt, her senses alert to every nuance of his body, from the scent of body-warmed cotton and tangy after-shave to the subtle pattern of his breathing. She had to lean close to mark the holes as he held the plywood against the door, and when her breast brushed his elbow, waves of reaction swept through her.

"What kind of perfume is that?" he asked as she marked the last hole.

She stood hastily and backed away, her heart thumping. "I don't wear perfume."

He lowered the plywood to rest on the floor. "Well, something makes you smell like a Christmas cookie." He stood and walked over to get the drill. Then he glanced at her. "Don't look so worried, Charity. Just because a man says you smell nice doesn't mean he's going to throw you to the floor and have his way with you." He crouched by the door again and shook his head. "Virgins."

"I am *not* a virgin!" she yelled above the sound of the drill, then cringed. Great, just great. Now he had her screaming out her sexual history.

He kept drilling, but his shoulders shook in what had to be a fit of laughter.

She waited until he was almost finished with the fourth hole. She'd show him, by God. He thought she was some inexperienced woman he could tease and torment with sexual references, but two could play at that little game. She picked up the small paper bag from the hardware store. Then she crouched next to him just as he laid down the drill.

"I know what you need, Wyatt," she murmured in a low, sultry voice.

He turned his head toward her, his expression suspicious. "Do you, now?"

"What you need is a good screw," she said softly.

His eyes widened in disbelief.

Holding his astonished gaze, she took his unresisting hand and turned it palm up. Then she dumped the contents of the bag into it. "There's four. Knock yourself out, cowboy." Gratified by his dazed look, she stood and left the room.

OH, BOY. Wyatt sat back on his heels and listened to Charity stomp out of the room. There was nothing more complicated than dealing with a woman who didn't know what she wanted. Especially when he wasn't too clear about what he wanted, either.

The television clicked on in the living room and Wyatt heard the measured voice of Peter Jennings presenting the evening news. He deposited the screws Charity had given him on the floor and reached for the screwdriver. If it weren't for the snowstorm he'd finish repairing the door and leave, which would certainly simplify the matter. But he couldn't leave. If the situation didn't feel like a setup, he just might have pushed the issue with Charity to see if he could tilt the scales in favor of fun and games. But Aunt Nora obviously wanted him to get involved with this woman. He'd bet on it. Which made Charity, whether she knew it or not, a trap.

He picked up the plywood and inserted the four screws, twisting each one into place with quick movements of the screwdriver. At first he'd thought Charity was a trap he could easily avoid. But she had a sneaky sexiness about her that was working on him. That was the only way to explain his uncharacteristic crack about virgins, which had turned up the heat several notches. Then she'd paid him back with an old joke that shouldn't have affected him at all. But coming from prim, buttoned-up Charity, it had packed a wallop.

With great effort he'd kept himself from lunging after her and easing the strain of their differences in a way they'd probably both find very satisfying. But in all likelihood that would spring Aunt Nora's trap.

Wyatt positioned the plywood and eased the protruding screws into the holes, noting with pleasure they were a snug fit. Using his shoulder to brace the wood, he tightened each screw in place. Finished. He stood and surveyed the job with pride. He'd forgotten how much fun he'd always had building or repairing things. Living out of motel rooms, he didn't have much call for that sort of skill.

"Good job," Charity said from somewhere behind him.

He turned in surprise at her conciliatory tone. "Thanks."

She made a vague gesture. We've gotten off to a bad start, you and I."

He noticed that she still held the television remote control. She must have turned off the TV and forgotten to put the remote down, which indicated just how preoccupied she was. "I guess you could call it a bad start," he said cautiously. He didn't quite trust this new friendliness. Or his reaction to her standing there, with her kissable mouth looking so soft and her cheeks flushing pink as his mother's spring roses.

She adjusted her large-frame glasses. "I usually don't...that is, I generally get along with the people I meet, both men and women."

"Me, too."

"In fact, people who know me say I'm good at making the best of a situation."

"Same here."

"But for some reason, around you I . . . find myself reacting in a way that's not like me at all." She hesitated. "I would hate for Nora to think that I . . ." She stopped, a pleading light in her blue eyes.

"Stop right there. I think we need an agreement." He smiled at her. "Considering we both have an image to protect, I won't tell Nora anything that's gone on between us if you'll return the favor."

She let out a breath and smiled back. "Deal."

A pact. The moment it was sealed he wondered at the wisdom of offering to link himself to her with shared secrets. They were already temporarily cut off from the world by the snowstorm, which would make them rely on each other more than normal. He was on treacherous ground and he'd better watch himself.

He reached for his jacket. "I'll put the tools back in the garage," he said more brusquely than the announcement warranted.

"And I'll see what we can do about dinner." Her tone was equally crisp.

He buttoned the jacket. "Don't go to any trouble."

"You're not hungry?"

In reality he was starving. All he'd had since breakfast was a bag of potato chips on the train. "Okay, then don't go to any trouble until I get back. I'll help you."

Her expression was filled with misgiving.

"What?" he asked, annoyed. "Don't you think I can handle myself in a kitchen?"

"To be honest, you don't look like the type," she said.

He picked up the tools. "Well, to be honest, neither do you."

The belligerence returned to her eyes. "And I suppose you judge a woman by her ability to cook?"

It had been a short truce, he thought. Exasperation made him reckless as he opened the kitchen door that connected to the garage. "No, I judge a woman by her ability in bed." He managed to get out the door before the remote hit it at the approximate level of his head. He opened the door a crack. "Good aim," he called before closing the door again.

SHE'D THROWN Nora's remote control. Charity stood in shock over the wreck. The case was cracked, the batteries scattered on the floor. She didn't throw things. She respected property, especially property belonging to someone else. That's why Nora had asked her to watch over the house.

Wyatt couldn't be held responsible for this, much as she'd like to blame it on him. She should know how to take taunts without responding like that. After all, she'd grown up with two younger brothers. She crouched, picked up the cracked remote, the batteries and the battery cover and carried them into the living room. With luck, it would still work so Nora would have something to use until Charity could buy her a new one.

Luck wasn't with her. No matter how she rearranged the batteries or in what order she pushed the buttons, the television remained blank and silent.

"Broken?" Wyatt leaned in the archway of the living room, his jacket unbuttoned, his Stetson shoved to the back of his head.

"Apparently." She clicked a few more times and sighed. "What a stupid thing to do."

Wyatt crossed to the ivory damask sofa. "Let me see."

She handed it to him and leaned her head back, her eyes closed. The sofa cushions shifted. She opened her eyes and turned her head.

He sat at the opposite end of the sofa, concentrating on the remote as he took off the battery cover and switched the batteries around. "I shouldn't have goaded you into it," he said without looking up. Then he lifted his gaze to hers and there was true regret there. "Sorry."

"I shouldn't have allowed myself to be goaded." She sat up straight again. "I'm supposed to be an adult."

A dimple flashed in his cheek. "Nobody's an adult all the time, Charity. And the world would be a dull place if they were." He tried the remote, but the television didn't respond. He took the battery cover off again.

Charity watched him put the batteries in a different order with a dexterity that surprised her. His hands were roughened and scarred by his profession, but his fingers remained nimble. She'd never had a chance to study a cowboy's hands before. A bull rider's hands, at that. "Do you usually wear gloves?" She hadn't meant to ask the question aloud.

He glanced up. "For remote control surgery? I don't think we have to worry about battery infection, do you?"

"For heaven's sake. I meant when you ride bulls."

"Oh. You should signal those turns, ma'am." He went back to examining the remote. "And to answer your question, I wear a glove on my weak hand, which is my left." He looked up again. "Why, are you thinking of taking up the sport? Not a lot of women, do, but believe it or not I can picture you battling it out with a Brahman." He pointed the remote at the television and clicked it vigorously.

"Was that some sort of crack?"

"No, ma'am, it was a compliment. You rode that doggy door real good."

"It was a crack!"

"Nope." He gazed at her. "Some women would have screamed and gotten hysterical in that kind of fix, but you didn't." He tossed the remote on the sofa between them. "And this is sure enough broken."

"Great."

"Look on the bright side. It's not an antique. Now let's head back into the kitchen." He levered himself from the sofa. "I'm starving."

Charity followed him. As she passed the powder room door she heard a whimper from inside. "Mac-Dougal!" With a rush of guilt she ran forward and wrenched open the door. "I forgot all about him!"

MacDougal surged out of the powder room and danced around her, his nails clicking on the pine floor.

"I'm so sorry, fuzz-face," she said, leaning down to scratch behind his ears. "I promise not to forget about you again." As she considered all the time he'd been cooped up she turned on the light in the little room to check for damage. When she looked inside, she gasped. Every surface was covered with unrolled toilet paper.

Wyatt looked over her shoulder and began to laugh. "A guy's got to amuse himself, right, Mac?"

The Scottie woofed.

"Look on the bright side," Wyatt added.

"I know, I know. The toilet paper wasn't antique." Charity glanced around the room to make sure nothing was permanently damaged. Deciding to clean it up later, she flicked off the light and closed the door. "There's been more destruction to this house in the past three hours than in the entire week I stayed here," she said as Wyatt continued down the hall into the kitchen.

"Are you implying something?"

"Well, nothing like this happened while I was here alone."

He reached the kitchen and turned to face her, his hands braced against his lean hips. "But since the big bad bull rider appeared, all hell has broken loose. Is that what you meant?"

She'd seen the light of challenge in his brown eyes enough to know another battle could easily follow, but she was too hungry to fight. "Let's just say we're a hazardous combination," she said.

"You'll get no argument from me on that. Do we have cheese?"

"Yes. We can toast some sandwiches."

"Great." Wyatt rummaged in the refrigerator and pulled out the cheese while Charity set up the electric skillet.

"Answer me honestly," Wyatt said as he began slicing cheese. "Do you think Nora intended to match us up over the holiday?"

Charity buttered the bread. "Well, she had invited me to Thanksgiving dinner."

"I'm not surprised."

"She didn't tell me you'd be here, either."

"Pretty suspicious behavior, wouldn't you say?"

"Suspicious and totally misguided." Charity laid the bread butter side down on the skillet and stepped back for Wyatt to arrange the slices of cheese on it. "Anyone can see we're exact opposites. We can't do anything together without arguing. What could she have been thinking?"

"God knows. Maybe she's getting mushy in her old age." He moved away from the skillet so Charity could put the buttered tops on the sandwiches. "Do we have any pickles to go with these?"

"Cucumber slices. I bought them this week."

"Perfect."

Charity's gaze slowly swiveled to his as she realized they'd just been working in complete harmony while making their dinner. He met her look, and her heart began to pound with a funny, hitching rhythm.

Finally he shrugged and looked away. "Nobody fights all the time."

Charity swallowed and tried to regain her composure. When Wyatt looked at her with that piercing intensity her insides got all tingly and liquid. She took a deep breath and smelled smoke. "The sandwiches are burning!" she cried, racing for a spatula.

"I knew you couldn't cook!" he snapped.

"Then why didn't you do it?"

He threw up both hands. "Because I figured you wanted to be in charge!"

"Men!"

"Women!"

The smoke alarm went off and MacDougal began to bark.

Wyatt looked at the blackened sandwiches and began to laugh. "At least we're back to normal around here."

4

A PERVERSE SENSE of humor made Charity insist they eat the charred sandwiches in the dining room, an elegant yet small space adjoining the living area. She used the dimmer switch on the crystal chandelier hanging over the lace-covered table and lit the white tapers rising majestically from pewter candlesticks created by Paul Revere.

She and Wyatt had debated whether to drink red or white wine with burned cheese sandwiches and had settled, surprisingly without much argument, on a bottle of cabernet. Charity had poured it into two goblets of hand-cut lead crystal and served the sandwiches on antique Spode china. In honor of the occasion Wyatt took off his hat and hung it on one of the dining room chairs. "I'm glad to see that Nora allows the candles to be burned," he said as he took a bite of his sandwich.

"She told me to use them if I wanted to, as long as I was careful." She tried not to fixate on a lock of brown hair that fell in sexy abandon over Wyatt's forehead. Bringing her attention back to dinner, she picked up her sandwich and took a tentative bite. It tasted like a charcoal briquet. She chewed and swallowed. "Delicious."

"Better than a mouthful of arena dirt." Without the hat shadowing his eyes, the twinkle was more visible.

"How sweet of you to say so."

"I suppose these plates and glasses are antiques."

Charity nodded. "Considering our track record, I'm probably tempting fate to bring them out, but I've been using her fine china all week. Nora does use her dishes and glassware."

"I know. I remember these plates." He glanced beside his chair where MacDougal whined and wriggled his stubby tail. "Hey, Mac, give it up. Trust me, you don't want a piece of this cheese sandwich anyway."

"He's not after your sandwich," Charity said.

"And I don't blame him. It tastes like a jogging shoe."

She gave him a withering glance because he probably expected her to, but he looked so good in the candlelight her heart wasn't really in it.

"A name-brand jogging shoe," he amended. "I'm so hungry I really don't care."

"I offered to make a new batch."

"Not with real conviction." He gave her an off center grin. "I figured things could get worse. Are you sure you want to tackle a turkey tomorrow?"

"A turkey is easy. You just stick it in a roaster and put it in the oven. Then you take it out when it's done."

"If you say so. I've never cooked one in my life."

Neither had Charity, but she'd be damned if she'd tell him that. The directions were printed right on the turkey wrapper, and she could read. "I tell you, it's a snap."

"Okay, but I—" Wyatt paused as the dog continued to whine. "What is it with you, Mac? I've never seen so much dedication to a cause."

"He wants the wine."

"No way. Dogs don't like wine."

Charity laughed. "This one does. Nora made the mistake of letting him taste some once, and he's been a fool for it ever since."

Wyatt stared at her. "And you give it to him?"

"Of course I don't give it to him! I'm here to take care of MacDougal, not get him drunk."

"Just asking. I want to make sure I understand all the rules. Speaking of which, am I allowed to have a second glass?"

"That's up to you, but I don't want anybody staggering around Nora's house endangering the Waterford crystal."

"I promise that two glasses of wine will not make me stagger."

Charity gestured toward the bottle. "Then help yourself."

"Thanks." He uncorked the bottle and held it up. "Any more for you?"

"No, thanks."

"In danger of staggering, Charity?"

"Of course not." She sounded priggish and didn't like the image. "Oh, all right. Half a glass."

"Stand back, folks. She's kicking over the traces. Next thing you know she'll be dancing naked on the table."

"Do you practice being obnoxious or does it just come naturally?"

He winked at her. "It's a gift. Come on, let's take our wine into the living room." He pushed back his chair.

"Don't sit on the white damask sofa with that red wine," she cautioned, following him.

"Then I'll sit on the rug."

"The rug's a hundred and twenty years old. I'm not sure a red wine stain would ever come out of it."

He made a face. "All this priceless stuff sure crimps a guy's style."

"And what style would that be, cowboy?" Charity chose an old Boston rocker.

Wyatt walked over to the frosty bay window, reached across the window seat and cleared one pane with a wipe of his sleeve. He gazed out into the snowy night as he sipped his wine. "Freedom, I guess."

She had to admit he looked a bit like a caged animal standing in the shadowed cave of the window staring out into the darkness. There was a restless set to his shoulders that clashed with a room designed for quiet pursuits like reading and needlepoint.

He turned and gestured around the room with the wineglass. "The opposite of all this."

Charity bristled at the implied criticism of a woman she idolized. "Nora had this place built for her, with no consideration of what a man would want in a house. That's pretty unusual, and I admire her for it."

"And you'd like to do the same someday?"

"Absolutely. Nora set the standard for me a long time ago."

"Really?" He walked out of the shadows by the window and moved toward her. "Just how long have you known my aunt?"

"I met her nineteen years ago, when I was ten. My mother brought me down from Boston for a feminist retreat Nora hosted in this house."

Wyatt nodded. "She was always big on feminism."

"And you're not?"

"I didn't say that. I believe in equal rights for women. But I resent being classified as the enemy just because I was born with different equipment between my legs than you have."

"Men have been classifying women that way for generations." Charity tried to convince herself they were having a political, not a sexual conversation. And she tried to keep her gaze from drifting below his belt. She failed on both counts. The heat of awareness swept through her as she considered, in detail, his "equipment."

"I had the feeling that you carry that sort of chip on your shoulder," he said.

She glanced upward into a chiseled face that attracted her far more than it should. She took refuge in rhetoric. "How can I not have a chip on my shoulder? I'm more likely to end up poverty-stricken than you, more likely to be raped, more likely to be—"

"Taken care of," he interrupted. "More likely to inherit the money accumulated by a man, because you'll live longer, on average. More likely to be—"

"Passed over for a promotion, to be defeated in an election," she countered.

MacDougal trotted between them and sat with his tongue out as his head swiveled from one to the other.

"He doesn't like confrontation," Charity said.

Wyatt crouched down and massaged MacDougal's spine. "No, he's a laid-back wino, aren't you, Mac?"

"Don't you dare give that dog any wine."

Wyatt looked at her, his gaze level with hers as he continued scratching the ecstatic Scottie. "Relax, Charity. I'm going to be a good boy."

Charity watched his supple fingers giving pleasure to the dog and almost wished he wouldn't be good. She had nothing, absolutely nothing, in common with this bull rider. But he was the sexiest man she'd met in a very long time.

WYATT STROKED the dog, but what he wanted desperately to do was stroke the woman, to take her hair out of its confining twist on top of her head, to remove the glasses as a prelude to removing a whole lot more. His urges astonished him. He wanted her not because she wore a seductive outfit, but because she didn't; not because she'd given him an unspoken invitation, but because she hadn't.

Their conversations inevitably became dueling matches, which should be a turnoff. Instead they heated his blood. Charity Webster represented everything he didn't want in a woman, and he desired her with a fierceness that made him tremble.

"Where am I sleeping?" he asked, deciding maybe they should end the evening before he lost control of his better judgment and kissed her.

"I put your duffel bag in the downstairs guest room."

He nodded as he continued to rub MacDougal's back. The dog closed his eyes in ecstasy. "That's where my parents used to sleep. I had the little bedroom upstairs, next to Nora's." He wondered if Charity had put them on separate floors on purpose. "You're taking Nora's room, then?"

"Yes."

He noticed the clipped answer, the flicker of heat in her gaze before she looked away. A carefully developed instinct told him that it wouldn't take much to lure her into his arms. Another glass of wine, perhaps. Some soft music on the stereo. A teasing invitation to dance.

Giving MacDougal a final pat, he stood. "I'll help you with the dishes, and then I think I'll turn in."

She stood, too, and finished the last of her wine. "Don't worry about the dishes. There's not much."

He could be imagining the regret in her tone, but somehow he didn't think so. Dammit, should he make a move? No. Charity was so different from the women he usually took to bed that he had a premonition the outcome might be different, too. That might be what Nora was after, but he didn't want to start anything that couldn't be finished quickly and cleanly, with no hurt feelings on either side.

"I'll help with the dishes," he said. "Otherwise you might accuse me of being a male chauvinist pig who's afraid of getting caught with his hands in a pan of soapsuds."

"Tell you what. You can take MacDougal to the backyard for his evening outing while I do the dishes."

That was so blatantly dividing up the jobs along gender lines that even Wyatt rebelled. "Are you afraid I'll break one of Nora's plates? Because I'll have you know I washed those same plates for her when I was fifteen, and I didn't break a single one." Actually, he'd broken two, which made the statement literally true. But he wasn't fifteen anymore. "Come on, Charity. You're so ready to trumpet the feminist cause. Put your money where your mouth is and take the dog out while I do up the dishes."

Her chin lifted. "Very well."

He almost laughed at her aristocratic response. Every time she got high-and-mighty with him, it made the prospect of penetrating that facade harder to resist. But he would resist, for his sake and hers.

CHARITY STOOD outside in the swirling snow and stomped her feet to keep warm. She jammed her hands into the pockets of her ski jacket and turned up the collar, but bits of snow still found their way down her neck

to bestow chilly kisses. Her green beret didn't do much
to keep her head warm, either. Out of habit she'd
brought MacDougal's leash, which was also stuffed into
her pocket. She hardly needed to worry about him running away on a night like this.

His coat must be protecting him pretty well, though,
she thought, because he floundered through the snow
chasing snowflakes and generally seemed uninterested
in doing what he'd been brought out to do. Charity
glanced over her shoulder through the kitchen window. It was fogged from the steam of hot dishwater, but
she could make out the hazy outline of Wyatt doing
dishes wearing his Stetson.

"This is ridiculous, Mac," she muttered, turning
back to the cavorting dog. "I'm the brains of this operation, so how come I end up with the worst job while
Wyatt's got it easy? I'm glad Nora's not here to see this
sorry turn of events."

MacDougal woofed and raced through a snowdrift.

"Come on, dog. Get down to business. You're going
to be sopping wet by the time we go back inside."

The Scottie ran to the other side of the yard and began barking at a bush.

"Hey! It's a bush! Nobody's out in this snowstorm
except you and me. So—" The rest of Charity's tirade
lodged in her throat as a shadow moved beside the bush.

"MacDougal, come!" she managed to gasp. The dog
trotted obediently toward her as she stared at the bush.
Keeping her attention on the shadow, she fumbled for
MacDougal's collar and snapped the leash into place.
The bulky figure shifted again, and she could swear it
emitted a cloud of steamy breath. It was way too big to
be a skunk or a raccoon. A bear? There weren't any
bears around Saybrook. Unless a bear had escaped

from a zoo somewhere. She jerked on Mac's leash and started backing toward the door. "Wyatt! Wyatt, come out here!"

Almost instantly he barreled out of the back door in his shirtsleeves, an apron tied around his jeans. "What? What's wrong?"

Holding tight to Mac's leash, she hurled herself into the safety of his arms, which enclosed her with reassuring strength. She'd never been so glad to see a protective alpha-male in her life. "S-something's out there." She looked up into his shadowy face. "Something like a b-bear."

"Take it easy." He sounded out of breath, and he wrapped her tighter in his arms. "It's okay. Where?"

"By the bush over there." She tilted her head in its direction. She could feel his heart pounding where her hand rested on his shirt. His nearness was so comforting she forgot to feel guilty about his being outside with no coat.

"I don't see anything."

"It was *there*. Mac was barking at it."

"Okay. Let's get you back inside. Then I'll take Mac out again and we'll investigate."

"Okay." She went inside, sheltered by his arm and chastened by her overwhelming gratitude that he was around to protect her. "Do you have your gun?"

"What gun?"

"Don't all cowboys have guns?"

"Not if they fly the friendly skies," he said as he ushered her inside and shut the door after them. "You'd have a devil of a time getting through the metal detector with a six-shooter strapped to your hip." Once they were inside he released her.

Immediately she missed the firm pressure of his arm around her and wanted it back. But that was idiocy. His arms around her now would create a danger inside the house greater than the one outside. "Well, you can't just go out there with nothing."

"Sure I can." He reached for his jacket. "I wouldn't take a gun out there even if I had one. I'd probably nail some neighbor's dog."

"If that was a dog, he's huge. And nobody's pet would be roaming the neighborhood in this weather." She noticed his damp shirt. "And you're all wet. You'll catch your death of cold."

Wyatt grinned at her as he buttoned his jacket. "Any more comments, or am I free to go?"

"Take something to defend yourself with. Take—" she glanced around the kitchen "—a rolling pin."

His dimple flashed. "No." He held out his hand for MacDougal's leash.

She handed it to him and for a brief moment their fingers met. She'd never been so aware of a simple, casual touch. She tried to keep the mocking tone in her voice. "What's the matter, would a rolling pin spoil your macho image?"

His probing glance held hers a second longer than necessary. He could probably see right through her attempt at bravado. "Yes, it would," he said. Then he wound the leash around his hand and opened the door. "Keep the home fires burning, Charity."

"Be careful," she called after him.

He poked his head back in the door. "Worried about me?"

"Wyatt Logan, you are not taking this seriously! There could be a serial killer out there, or a wild animal escaped from the zoo, or an inmate from the state mental hospital, or—"

"An alien from outer space?" he asked with mock seriousness.

"Go on, then! Get yourself killed."

"Thanks for the vote of confidence, ma'am." He touched the brim of his hat and closed the door.

Charity wrenched it open again. "Just don't expect me to retrieve the body!" she shouted after his retreating back.

He kept walking into the snowy yard. "Well, Mac, she just eliminated the element of surprise. Now we'll have to use our brute strength to overpower those aliens."

INSIDE HIS HOUSE, Alistair's heart slammed against his ribs when Charity's words blasted through his earphones. *Don't expect me to retrieve the body!* Nora's body. It was lying somewhere, unburied. He had to find out where. He'd read enough Patricia Cornwell mysteries to know that the authorities found all sorts of evidence on the body.

It had taken him a good hour to plant a bug just outside Nora's back door. Or as close to a bug as he could manage—the microphone from his karaoke machine. He'd commandeered every length of connecting wire in the house, which meant dismantling his surround-sound system.

He'd barely finished burying the wires in the snow and almost hadn't made it into hiding behind that bush when Charity had unexpectedly come outside with the dog, but the near discovery had been worth it. He already had Charity on tape claiming to be the brains of the operation. Then, typical of a woman like that, she'd refused the messy job of retrieving Nora's body.

The nephew was obviously the hitman, but the plot had apparently been hatched by none other than Charity Webster, Nora's trusted friend and protégée. Alistair sighed. 'Twas ever thus. In his experience, good deeds seldom went unpunished.

5

WYATT DIDN'T EXPECT to find anything amiss in the backyard, but he dutifully took Mac around the perimeter, figuring that the dog would alert him to anything unusual. Mac seemed unconcerned. Then, to cover all bases, Wyatt trudged through the side yard to the front, his boots sinking in snow nearly a foot deep.

It was damned cold out, but fresh and clean. Snow was a treat for an Arizona boy, and he held out his hand to allow the flakes to light on his palm like butterflies. Then he looked straight up, and the flakes seemed to hurl themselves past him like tiny asteroids traveling at warp speed.

He wasn't going to rush this tour of duty. He needed some time to think. When he returned to the house he'd better know for sure how he intended to proceed. When Charity had called for him he'd raced outside, where the cold had slammed the breath from him. What little breath he had left had been stolen as she'd thrown herself into his arms. Her Christmas-cookie scent had caught him off guard, and when she'd lifted her face, pink from the cold, he'd come very close to kissing her.

He hadn't given in, because if he did kiss her, he wanted it to be part of a conscious decision, not some accidental embrace. If he was confused about many aspects of this crazy situation, he was dead sure of one thing. A kiss would only be the beginning. When he walked in that door, he should be ready to take her in his arms and follow through or go straight to his own bedroom and stay there.

After making his way to the backyard again, he unhooked MacDougal's leash and let the dog roam. Wyatt positioned himself with his back to the door and surveyed the snowy landscape for any sign of intruders. There were none. Charity's imagination had been working overtime. But imagination could be a good thing in certain situations—when two people were tucked beneath a fluffy comforter, for example.

A sweet ache built within him, defying the cold. Staring into the swirling snow, he pictured Charity with her hair down, her glasses laid aside, her high-necked blouse unbuttoned.... He fantasized the gentle pop of her bra fastening as it gave way, revealing the breasts hidden beneath silk and lace, and her vanilla scent growing stronger as he leaned forward to press his lips against her creamy skin.

Then he heard, in real time, the back door open. He wondered if she could have somehow tuned into his thoughts and was about to beckon him inside. Perhaps she'd already taken her hair down in preparation for—

"Did you see anything out there?" she called.

He turned.

Her hair was in place, her blouse buttoned up to her neck.

"No," he said.

"Well, I'm going to bed. Lock up when you come in, will you?"

So much for thinking he was the one in charge of the decision. While he'd pictured her inside pacing the floor in a turmoil of frustration, she'd probably been upstairs brushing and flossing her teeth. Whoever said women were the more romantic sex hadn't met Charity Webster.

"Come on, Mac." Wyatt turned toward the house. "It's been a hell of a long day."

INTENSE COLD woke Charity in the pale light of early dawn. Then she smelled smoke. The alarm must have failed. Wearing one of Nora's flannel nightgowns, she leapt from the double bed, grabbed her glasses from the nightstand and ran out into the upstairs hall, her sock feet skidding on the wood floor. By the time she reached the landing she was awake enough to remember MacDougal and Wyatt, in that order.

"Fire!" she shrieked. "Everybody up! Everybody outside!"

Barking furiously, MacDougal raced from the living room and up the stairs toward her. Then Wyatt, dressed in cream-colored sweatpants and sweatshirt, appeared at the bottom of the stairs.

"Help me get the dog out," Charity ordered as she started down. "We have a fire."

"I know." Wyatt crossed his arms and looked up at her. His beard-stubbled chin made him look more masculine than ever. "I built it."

Charity grabbed the banister and came to an abrupt halt. "Where?"

"In the middle of the living room."

She gave him an uncomprehending stare.

"Not really. I guess it's a little early in the morning for jokes. I built a fire in the fireplace. We don't have any—"

"You did *what?*" She started down the stairs again. "Put it out right now, Wyatt. I realize you want more holiday atmosphere, but—"

"We don't have any power. The furnace is dead. It's our only source of heat now."

So that's why the house was so bitter cold. "Dammit. Have you looked outside?"

He nodded. "I had to scrape the window to do it. Near as I can tell, the snow's at least five feet deep, with drifts higher than that. I got the back door open, finally, to find a wall of snow packed against it."

Charity groaned.

"It looks kind of neat, to be honest. I found a shovel in the garage and dug a little cave for MacDougal to go out this morning."

"Well, thank you for doing that. Did you try the telephone?"

"Dead."

Charity sank to a sitting position on the steps and put her head in her hands. Wyatt might think the whole thing was a great adventure, but she had the ultimate responsibility for the house. "All I wanted was to keep this house neat and orderly until Nora got back," she moaned. "Now the door's busted, her remote's broken, we're snowed in and the fireplace will be scorched."

"If you're going to complain about the situation you might as well come down and do it in front of the fire. It's much nicer there."

She lifted her head in sudden dismay. "Nora didn't have a supply of firewood."

"I know. I had to chop up the Hepplewhite. It was blocking the path to the back door anyway."

She evaluated the dancing light in his brown eyes. "That's not very funny." But she stood just in case he was telling the truth, so she could rush into the living room and save what was left of the antique furniture.

"I thought it was funny, but maybe you Eastern folks need caffeine before you can find your sense of humor."

"Coffee would help. I'll make some."

He smiled. "Can I watch?"

She put her hands on her hips. "Look, I may have scorched the cheese sandwiches, but I can certainly measure coffee and plug in...." She paused. "Oh."

"I was afraid to hang the coffee maker over the campfire."

She glared at him. "You never answered my question. What are you burning?"

"I rummaged around in the garage and found some old wood stacked in the rafters. Probably left over from a remodeling job or something."

"You're sure it's scraps?"

"Come and look."

Wrapping her arms around herself she followed him into the living room where, sure enough, a lusty fire crackled in the marble fireplace. Next to it was a stack of nondescript boards that had been split into fireplace-size pieces. "They were just stacked in the rafters?" she asked. "A pile of old wood?"

Wyatt held up a hand. "Scout's honor. Listen, we needed something to keep us warm. It's always possible Aunt Nora planned to do something decorative with that old wood, but right now, heat is more important. She'll understand that. I'm sure she can get more just like it. Connecticut is full of that stuff."

"I want to see the rest." Charity walked to the garage door and opened it. A wave of cold engulfed her, but she stepped into the gasoline-scented interior and automatically reached for the light switch next to the door. Nothing happened.

"No power," Wyatt reminded her.

"Thank you, Mr. Wizard." She opened the door of the Mercedes and light filtered from the dome light upward into the rafters.

"Ingenious," Wyatt said.

Charity didn't answer as she peered upward at the cobwebbed boards above her.

"Looks like junk to me," Wyatt commented from the doorway.

"I guess you're right." With only a flannel nightgown and socks to protect her against the vicious cold, she began to shiver uncontrollably.

"Come inside, Charity, before you catch your death."

She turned, her teeth chattering. "Worried about me?"

"Yes." He caught her arm and pulled her back through the door. "Nora seems to set great store by you for some unknown reason, and I don't want to be blamed for anything that happens to you while I'm around." He released her the minute they closed the garage door. She continued to shake. "Come on," he said with a resigned air and took her hand to pull her toward the living room.

"I s-should get d-dressed," she managed to say around her shivers.

"Get warmed up first." He placed her in front of the fire. "Sit."

She sank to her knees in grateful submission to his order and held out her hands to the heat. A few moments later he draped a quilt over her shoulders. She looked at it and recognized the antique quilt from the downstairs guest room. "We probably shouldn't be using this in front of the fire," she said. "In case of sparks."

He squatted beside her. "We have an emergency situation, here. Would you rather they found our frozen bodies in the midst of an undisturbed decorating scheme?"

"You're overreacting. Nobody—"

"Wanna bet?" He glanced at her. "Out in Arizona we read about it all the time. Power out for days, people dying of the cold. That's not going to happen to us if I can help it."

"The power won't be out for days. I hope." In truth she had no idea what to expect. She'd never lived in such a rural area before.

"In all the disaster movies they assume the worst and prepare for that," Wyatt said. "Of course then the worst always happens."

"What a wonderful comfort you are." She snuggled into the quilt and decided not to argue right now. The sensation of warming up after being near frozen was so delicious she didn't want to disturb the cozy feeling. MacDougal wiggled in between her and Wyatt and plopped down, his head on his paws.

As she gradually warmed up, Charity began to consider the situation more fully. "We may have a bit of a problem here," she said, glancing at Wyatt.

"Somehow I sensed that," he said with a wry grin. "How much?"

"The entire house is electric now. Nora was very proud of that."

"I don't suppose there's a backup generator?" he asked with a slight trace of hope.

Charity shook her head. "She'd talked about it, but then she became involved in a few other projects and never got around to installing one."

"That sounds like her." Wyatt reached down to scratch behind MacDougal's ears. "She has a reputation for getting sidetracked. Once she bought a little boat but never did get oars or a motor for it. My dad finally took care of buying a motor one summer."

"It's because she has more lofty things on her mind," Charity said. "I've never known someone so generous and ready to help others, especially women in tough situations. If it weren't for Nora, I'd be back in New York working for one of the big bookstore chains right now."

Wyatt continued scratching MacDougal, who by now had stretched out full length, enjoying the attention and warmth. "I figured she must have given you some financial backing."

"At a critical time. I'd saved enough to make the down payment on the store, but I needed to show a profit in order to stay in business. Because I was one of the few bookshops in the area, I thought business would pour in immediately. It didn't, except for Alistair Updegraff and Nora."

"So you weren't kidding about Updegraff being a valued customer."

"Absolutely not." With growing envy, Charity watched MacDougal enjoying Wyatt's caress. The night before she'd summoned the resolve to avoid Wyatt's charms, but her resolve had disappeared with the morning light.

"What does he buy?"

"Nothing but mysteries." Charity turned her attention to the leaping flames in an attempt to take her mind off the erotic images of Wyatt's fingers giving her the kind of pleasure MacDougal was receiving. "Everything from Agatha Christie to Sue Grafton. He has a cape and hat that make him look like Sherlock Holmes. For a while he tried to smoke a pipe to complete the image, but he got sores on his tongue and had to give it up."

Wyatt laughed. "He's a real piece of work. He seems to think I should be thrilled because I'm Nora's only heir."

"He would think like that. He's always fooling with his own will."

"He has kids?"

"Two sons, neither one married. Maybe they're both licking their chops over their inheritance. I never could understand people who put great importance on inheriting money."

"Me, either. It's a waste of time. I figure Aunt Nora will leave all hers to the National Organization for Women, or Mac, here, if he outlives her."

"After what she's done for me, she can light candles with it and I'll support her decision," Charity said. "She walked in the day I was putting up the Going Out Of Business sign and immediately offered me a loan, no strings attached. So you see, if I succeed, I'll owe it all to Nora." She turned her head to gaze at Wyatt. "I'd go to the wall for that woman."

He smiled. "I think you're about to be put to the test. She asked you to cook me a turkey for Thanksgiving."

"But the stove's out of commission."

"There's always the fireplace."

"To cook a turkey? Hey, I don't know if I can cook one in a regular oven, let alone over an open fire!"

Amusement danced in his eyes. "Aren't you the one who said last night that it was a snap?"

And so she had. She met his gaze defiantly. "I was planning to follow the directions on the wrapper."

"I see. That isn't quite the same as being an old hand, though, is it?"

"A gentleman wouldn't look so smug about catching me in a little fib."

The light in his eyes changed subtly. "I never claimed to be a gentleman, Charity." He didn't look like one, either, with that gleam in his eye and the shadow of a beard darkening his cheeks and chin.

As he continued to gaze at her she became self-conscious for the first time since she'd barreled out into the hall yelling about the fire. She'd been sitting here talking to him with no makeup on, her hair loose and disheveled, and nothing on under her flannel nightgown. She stood and wrapped the quilt closer around her. "I think it's time for me to get dressed."

He pushed himself to his feet. "Why?"

"I—"

"I don't think we'll have company today, do you?"

"Maybe Nora will come back." It was an idle statement and she knew it. Nothing was moving outside, not even a snowplow.

"She won't be back today." He paused, as if to give his next comment more significance. "Probably not tonight, either."

Her heart began to race. He was making sure she understood that she was snowbound with him for the rest of the day...and the rest of the night. "How do you know? You don't even live around here."

"Come and look." He guided her with a gentle hand on her shoulder over to the bay window where he'd scratched a peephole in the frosty glass. He wiped it again with his sleeve and gestured her forward.

She leaned over the window seat and looked out an opening about the size of a baseball. Then she drew in a quick breath. Nothing outside was recognizable. The drifts were at eye level, and the whole world looked as if it had been dipped in marshmallow topping. There was no street, no mailbox, no bushes. Only the tall pines and maples reached above the blanket of silent snow. Charity had lived all her life in the East, yet she'd never seen anything quite like this. It must be the storm of the century.

Slowly she turned back to Wyatt as the implications of total isolation with this man tripped her pulse into double time. "You're right." She sounded far more casual than she felt. "We're cut off from the rest of the world, probably until tomorrow, at least."

"I may even have a problem getting back to Madison Square Garden for the rodeo on Saturday."

"Surely the trains will be running by then."

"Probably, but we're definitely out of the loop for now." There was an unmistakable suggestion in his gaze. "For better or worse, we're on our own." He stepped closer, and she held her breath.

"Help me!" shouted a voice from somewhere in the front of the house.

Wyatt paused. "Then again, maybe not."

"It's Alistair!" Charity turned back to look out the window as the cry for help came again. "But I can't see him!" She threw off the quilt and raced for the stairs.

Wyatt followed her. "What are you doing?"

"We can see better from Nora's bedroom balcony. Come on."

"I'm right behind you."

In the bedroom Charity pulled back the drapes covering the French doors onto the balcony. The balcony roof had partly protected the area, and the snow was only about a foot deep on the deck. Charity clicked open the dead bolt, turned the knob and pulled, but nothing happened.

"It's frozen shut." Wyatt stood so close behind her she could feel his warm breath on her neck. "Let me try."

She stood back while the cries from Alistair continued. At least there was nothing wrong with Alistair's lungs. As the cold penetrated her flannel nightgown she began to shiver again.

Wyatt braced himself, took hold of the handle, and heaved. The door came open with a loud crack. "Stay here." He glanced back at her. "I'll go look. And for God's sake, put on a bathrobe or something."

She glanced down and noticed that her nipples, reacting to the cold, jutted sharply beneath the soft flannel. As she hurried toward Nora's closet she wondered if that had been what had put the edge in Wyatt's voice. She grabbed a heavy fleece robe. As she jammed her feet into fur-lined boots sitting on the floor of the closet, she heard Wyatt shouting down to Alistair and Alistair calling something back, but she couldn't understand what either man was saying.

By the time she started toward the French doors Wyatt was heading back inside, his sweatpants soaked up to his knees from the snow.

"What's his problem?" Charity asked.

Wyatt looked as if he was using all his restraint not to laugh. "He's buried up to his family jewels in a snow-drift. I'll be right back."

"Where are you going?"

"To get my rope."

6

WYATT PULLED HIS ROPE, his rosin bag and a left-hand glove out of his duffel bag before heading back upstairs. He hoped Nora's balcony was built well enough to support the weight of a man the size of Alistair Updegraff. What a guy. Tried to sneak over on antique snowshoes. Apparently old snowshoe webbing stretched like a rubber band once it got wet.

When he got back to the balcony, Charity was already out there kicking snow out of the way. Pale sunlight crept beneath the balcony roof to give her blond hair a subtle glow. In the fluffy white robe, and outlined against the snow blanketing the landscape, she looked like an angel—an angel in large-framed glasses, which made the picture uniquely Charity. She was becoming entirely too attractive for comfort.

"I might need some packed snow for traction," he said as he came to join her.

She lowered her voice. "You're not really going to rope him, are you?" Little puffs of steam escaped her mouth as she talked, caressing his face.

He ducked his head and muffled his response. "How else am I going to get him out of that drift?"

"And then what?"

"Well, we can either pull him up to the balcony, in

which case he'll probably be here all day...." He glanced sideways at Charity.

She shook her head vigorously, making her blond hair fly around her shoulders.

Well, at least she didn't want a built-in chaperone. That was something. He longed to run his fingers through her loose hair, but this wasn't exactly the time. "Or we can swing him like a pendulum so he can grab the railing of his front porch and climb onto that," he said.

Charity gasped. "I don't think he's agile enough for stunts, Wyatt."

"Hey, Charity!" Alistair called from beneath them. "Would you two quit playing around up there and do something? I haven't got all day, you know."

Charity exchanged a glance with Wyatt.

"Or we can leave him to freeze his buns off," Wyatt said.

Charity sighed. "Tempting, but we can't and you know it."

He grinned at her. "Your customer. Your call."

"Hey, people, any day now. It's very *cold* down here," Alistair remarked in a loud voice.

Charity looked at Wyatt again. "Swing him."

Wyatt uncoiled his rope. "I thought you'd see it that way." He leaned over the balcony. "Here's the plan, Updegraff. I'll throw a loop around you. Fix it under your armpits, and—"

"You are going to lasso me?" Alistair squeaked.

"That's the way we handle things out West," Wyatt said, biting his lip to keep from chuckling. The wooden frame of the snowshoes rested on top of the drift. It looked as if Alistair had been slam-dunked into a pair of irregular basketball hoops.

"Well, I don't fancy being roped like some prize heifer!" Alistair said. "Think of something else, cowboy."

Wyatt turned his back to the railing and spoke to Charity in a low tone. "A prize heifer would get more consideration from me. This guy's beginning to get on my nerves."

"Tell me about it. I've been dealing with his prissy little preoccupations for a week. But we have to do our best, Wyatt. He can't stay there, after all."

Wyatt sighed and turned back to Alistair. "Trust me, this is the most efficient way to get you out of there. Once the rope is under your armpits, I'll pull you out of the drift and Charity will snub the rope around this post."

"Oh, yeah, and then what?" Alistair said.

Charity tugged on his arm. "Will the post hold?" she whispered.

"Just a second, Updegraff." Wyatt lowered his voice again as he spoke to Charity. "I'll try to take most the weight myself, but if the worst happens and I lose my grip, the post would help break his fall."

"And break," Charity said.

"I think Nora would rather replace the post than have us damage Alistair."

"Can I help hold the rope?"

"How much experience do you have with ropes?"

"None."

"Then you could get hurt. Just wrap it around the post once I get him airborne." He turned back to the stranded neighbor. "Okay, Updegraff, when you're free of the snow, you'll automatically start to swing—"

"Oh, sure! You'd like to have me swinging at the end of your rope, wouldn't you? If you think I'll go for that, you've got another think coming, Mr. Rodeo Star.''

Wyatt threw up his hands. "Okay. Have it your way. We'll be inside sitting by a toasty fire if you change your mind. Come on, Charity."

She resisted the tug of his hand. "But, Wyatt, we can't—"

"He'll cave."

"Wait!" Alistair called.

Wyatt lifted an eyebrow at Charity. "See?" Then he turned and walked back to the balcony railing. "As I was saying, you'll automatically start swinging toward this house. Push off when you get here, and the motion should bring you back to a spot where you can grab your porch railing."

"Why not just pull me on up there with you?"

Because then Charity and I wouldn't be alone, and I'm beginning to love that idea, Wyatt thought. "We've got stomach flu over here, Updegraff," he said. "The really nasty kind from one of those Oriental cities— Hong Kong, Singapore, something like that."

"And you're handling a rope that you plan to throw at me? You're planning to spew flu germs in my direction, is that it?"

"I washed my hands real good."

Looking more like a peg-person than ever with his legs buried in the snow, Alistair folded his arms. "I guess I don't have a choice, do I?"

"Nope," Wyatt answered. "And remember, I'm a professional. Don't try this at home."

"That's not funny."

Wyatt turned to Charity and tried to look wounded. "Nobody gets my jokes. I'm beginning to develop a complex."

She made a face. "As if you ever would."

Wyatt grinned and rubbed his rosin bag over both palms before pulling on his glove. He was used to lacing it himself by using his teeth, but Charity stepped forward.

"I can do that, at least."

"Okay." He held out his hand and she leaned over to concentrate on the task. Wyatt had the compelling urge to place a kiss on her golden hair.

She looked up at him with endearing sincerity. "How's that?"

When she wasn't up on her high horse about something, she was quite a temptation, he thought. But then she was a temptation when she was taunting him, too. He flexed his fingers in the glove. "That's great. Thanks."

She smiled with pleasure and his breath caught at the beauty of it.

Time to get his mind back on the business at hand, he decided. He picked up his rope, built the loop and leaned over the balcony so he could get a good arc with the toss.

"Be careful," Charity said.

"I'm always careful."

"Coming from a man who rides bulls as a living, that lacks a certain ring of truth."

He should have known she couldn't stay sweet for long, but that was okay. He liked this version of her, too. He aimed for the fluorescent orange pom-pom on Alistair's knit cap. "Just remember, Charity, when you're bad-mouthing my profession, that it took a rodeo man to rescue your valued bookstore customer." He settled his loop neatly around Alistair's torso.

"Not too bad." Her voice contained a grudging note of admiration.

"Tighten it under your arms," Wyatt shouted to Alistair. "That's it. Hold on to the rope and kick free as soon as you can. Now, get ready. I'm going to start pulling you up."

Wyatt braced his feet against the base of the balcony railing, took a deep breath, and started the hand-over-hand process. At first he just dragged Alistair through the snow a bit, but eventually the little man began to rise from the bank as Wyatt pulled, breathing hard. His shoulders began to ache from the strain and he wondered if this was such a great idea two days before a very important rodeo competition. He kept pulling.

As Alistair's feet cleared the snow, the limp snow-shoe webbing dangled from his boots, which made it look as if Alistair had started unraveling. Wyatt was clenching his jaw too hard to enjoy the sight. His entire upper body burned from the effort. He braced himself for the upward pull, but when Alistair began to swing, Wyatt realized he might be drawn sideways on the slick balcony surface.

"Should I wrap the rope around the post now?" Charity asked.

"Yep." Wyatt put his back into one last heave.

With a bad imitation of a Tarzan yell, Alistair began to swing.

"Tie it and come hang on to me," Wyatt said through gritted teeth. "Or I might slide sideways when he swings back toward his house."

"That would be bad?"

"If the post goes, I'd go with it."

"That would be bad."

Wyatt tended to agree.

Charity hurried over to him and wrapped her arms around his waist.

"Hold tight. He's swinging back toward his porch." Sweat dripped down Wyatt's face as he tried to control the rope. Below him Alistair sailed toward his target, the collapsed snowshoes trailing after him and bumping along on the drifts.

"We could make a fortune on 'America's Funniest Home Videos' with this," Charity said into his ear.

"When it's over I plan to laugh myself silly," Wyatt gasped.

Alistair swung lazily toward the rail and reached out a hand just as Wyatt, even with Charity's extra weight, started slipping toward the post. Wyatt had a split second to choose between risking Charity or Alistair. He let go of the rope.

In the same second Wyatt and Charity tumbled backward in a heap, the rope snapped tight around the post, pulling it loose from its moorings. As the balcony roof sagged, snow cascaded like a waterfall, obscuring the view of Alistair's fate.

Wyatt found his legs tangled with Charity's, but he'd instinctively kept his full weight from landing on her. Breathing hard, he eased up on one elbow to look down into her astonished gaze. Her glasses had been knocked halfway across the balcony, but from here they didn't look broken. "Sorry about that." He gulped for air. "It was him or us. You okay?"

"Yes. Are you?"

"I think so."

"Alistair. Is he—"

"I made it!" shouted Alistair from below.

Wyatt heaved a sigh of relief. "He's okay."

"No thanks to you two!" Alistair added. "You almost got me killed!"

Wyatt looked down at Charity. "It's so nice to be appreciated, don't you think?"

"The post gave way, didn't it?" she asked.

"Afraid so, but look on the bright side. It wasn't an—"

"An antique," Charity finished, and began to smile.

When her smile turned to a chuckle, Wyatt was drawn in, and soon both of them were laughing uncontrollably.

"Don't think I can't hear you up there!" Alistair called. "Having sport with me! I don't believe you told me the truth about the Hong Kong flu, either."

Charity and Wyatt paused, glanced at each other, and burst out laughing again.

"I'll never forget the way he looked when . . ." Charity kept her voice down and tried to control herself. "When you hauled him up with those sorry snowshoes dangling down . . ." She dissolved into a new fit of giggles.

"Did you hear the Tarzan yell?" Wyatt whispered, choking on another wave of laughter.

"He thinks . . . he's got a great voice," Charity said, gasping. "In the summer he leaves the windows open and belts out old show tunes. He has one of those karaoke things hooked to his stereo."

"You're making that up."

"He does. Nora swears to it."

Wyatt grinned. "Thank God, it's November."

"Nora claims his rendition of *Oklahoma* has put her off Rodgers and Hammerstein forever. By the way, can you see my glasses anywhere? I'm blind as a bat without them."

"Yeah. Right over here." He reached across her to pick up the glasses, which brought them almost into an embrace. He heard her quick intake of breath and his pulse beat a little faster. "They look fine," he said, trying to act nonchalant. He'd suddenly become aware of how close she was, lying there practically underneath him.

He held the glasses by the earpiece, meaning to return them to her, but he hesitated. Gazing down at Charity, her cheeks glowing and her eyes bright, he decided he'd never seen anything so tempting in all his thirty-two years. His muscles ached, his knee hurt where he'd fallen, and melting snow was soaking slowly but surely into his sweat suit. He didn't care. He laid the glasses down again. "Hold still," he murmured.

A look of concern replaced her amusement. "Why? Is something wrong?"

"No. Something's finally right." As he leaned down he watched concern become knowledge in her blue eyes. Then anticipation.

His heart thundered in his ears. "Can you see me better now?" he murmured.

Her throat moved in a tiny swallow. "I'm a whiz at close-ups."

"Then maybe that's where I need to stay."

"I don't think this is a very good idea, Wyatt."

"Gonna stop me, Miss Charity?"

Her throat moved again. "No," she murmured.

"Good." Then he closed his eyes and gave himself up to the sensation of kissing Charity. Her mouth tasted the way he'd imagined it might—sweetly subtle, with passion hiding behind a barrier of caution. He brushed his lips across hers to enjoy the velvet texture and the cushioning fullness before he pressed deeper, coaxing her to open to him. She did, but slowly, and he angled his head to gain what he wanted.

His tongue claimed possession gently, without rushing, at last taking advantage of her sigh of surrender to explore the moist heat of her mouth. And that heat was building. She spread her fingers over the back of his head and pulled him deeper, slackening her jaw in deliberate provocation. He cupped her cheek with his left hand, then cursed inwardly because he still wore the leather glove.

Amazingly, the touch of the worn leather seemed to bring her to a greater level of excitement. Moaning softly, she twisted more fully beneath him, arching upward. Only a fool would resist an invitation like that, and Wyatt was no fool. Pushing aside her robe, he unfastened the top buttons of the nightgown with clumsy movements of his gloved hand. When he slipped his hand inside and cupped her fullness, she gasped against his mouth.

As he kneaded her soft breast and wished he could eliminate the barrier of the glove, her kiss became more frenzied, her breathing more ragged. She was wild for him. He grew hard at the thought of making love to her right here, pushing her nightgown up and just....

But then understanding dawned. The glove was having this effect. It wasn't him she wanted so much as a rough and rugged rodeo cowboy. Disappointment mingled with his arousal. He lifted his mouth a fraction as his hand closed completely over her breast, squeezing it. "If it's leather you like," he whispered, "maybe I should wear my chaps when we make love. And bring my rope."

She grew very still. "Get away from me this second," she said, panting with the remnants of passion, "or so help me, I'll turn you into a soprano, buster."

Breathing hard, he rolled away, right into a mound of snow. "Oh, jeez." But she'd been in a perfect position to knee him in the crotch and he didn't think she was too squeamish to do it. "Damn, this stuff is cold." Wiping snow from his face, he sat up and glared across at her. He held up his left hand. "And I suppose this leather glove had nothing to do with your response just now?"

She tugged her nightgown together and struggled to a sitting position. "You're so insulting."

"Maybe I was a little insulted, too." Despite himself his gaze drifted to her mouth, reddened by his kisses, and his body stirred anew. He shouldn't have said anything, just helped himself. Did it matter whether he was her token rodeo cowboy if he got some pleasure in exchange? It wasn't as if that hadn't been the deal many times before, with other women. He couldn't understand why it bothered him so much now.

"I'm going inside." She tried to get up, but slipped on the wet balcony and would have fallen smack on her fanny if he hadn't leaned over and grabbed her by the elbow, steadying her descent.

He guided her gently back to the balcony floor. "Need some help getting up?" he asked.

She pulled away from him. "No, thank you."

"Okay." He sat back, his arms wrapped around his bent knees and watched.

Her problem was that she was trying to protect her modesty while she got to her feet, but the nightgown and bathrobe kept riding up on her, and when she'd tug it back down she'd lose her balance on the slippery surface. Finally she made it up, but not before Wyatt had been treated to several delicious glimpses of her creamy calves and thighs.

She stomped through the French doors into Nora's bedroom without a backward glance. She closed the door with an angry snap of her wrist. Then she closed the drapes. She pulled the cord with such energy that the drapes swung from the impact for several seconds afterward.

Observing this display of temper, Wyatt wondered if she'd turn the dead bolt, as well. He listened for the click. If it came, he'd just have to break in, but he'd rather not do any more damage to Nora's house than necessary. He glanced at the sagging roof over the balcony and the post pulled out of position by his rope. Maybe he could shove the post back into position, but it would have to be repaired sometime.

When no sound of locks turning came from the door, Wyatt concluded that Charity understood that locking him out wouldn't do any good. At least she'd figured out that much about him.

Wyatt decided to sit in the slush a little longer. His shoulders and arms could use heat and massage, but what he was sitting in was perfect for easing that other ache, the one that wouldn't be getting any relief soon, if Charity had anything to do with it.

7

ALISTAIR SELDOM resorted to blasphemy. He considered it a sign of insufficient vocabulary skills. But as he propped himself on his front porch railing to rid himself of the tangle that had once been snowshoes, he allowed himself one muttered, "Dammit." He'd found the confounded things in a trunk packed years ago by his dear, departed Cordelia. He'd never been on snowshoes in his life, but in these dire circumstances they'd seemed like a gift from above. Apparently they'd been a curse from below, instead.

Fortunately he'd layered himself with two pairs of thermal underwear and two pairs of socks before he'd put on his ski pants and boots, so the time he'd spent half submerged in a snowbank hadn't given him frostbite. A man who failed to plan was a man who planned to fail, he'd told both his sons more than once. They'd each made use of that advice in their careers with military intelligence.

He could have used his sons' expertise in this caper, as a matter of fact, but he seemed to be managing fine on his own. Swinging on the rope had been quite exhilarating until the nephew had let it go and he'd smacked up against the railing spread-eagled like one of those characters in a Roadrunner cartoon. Thank heavens he'd been able to grab the rail at the last minute instead of falling backward into the snow.

They were a devilish pair, those two, cackling away up on the balcony after they thought they'd finished him off. But Alistair Updegraff was tougher than that, by golly. Maybe the loss of electrical power had knocked out his carefully placed listening device, but he'd find some other way to collect his evidence.

He still had his telescope, and his bedroom window was exactly opposite Nora's. If they hadn't pulled the shade down on that window he might be able to see something interesting. He'd also continue to study *Sleuthing Tips*, so chock-full of ideas gleaned over the years from his panel of experts—Miss Marple, Hercule Poirot, Sherlock Holmes, and of course his beloved Jessica Fletcher. What an astounding think tank! Charity Webster and Wyatt Logan had no idea what they were up against.

CHARITY TOOK Nora's boots and robe off as soon as she closed the drapes. MacDougal danced around her in pleasure, welcoming her back.

"Stay back, fuzz-face, until I can deal with this mess," she ordered. Everything she had on was sopping wet, but the robe had soaked up the melted snow like a sponge and was dripping. She bundled it in her arms and carried it into Nora's bathroom, where she dumped it in the tub. MacDougal followed her and cocked his head, looking puzzled.

Charity reached down to give him a pat. "Your world is upside down, too, isn't it? Oh, Mac, what I wouldn't give for a long, hot bath." And the privacy to enjoy it, she thought. She tried the tap and discovered not even cold water came out. This power outage was turning into a bigger hassle than she'd originally expected.

Shivering, she returned to Nora's closet and found a pink sweat suit. After going back inside the bathroom to put the suit on, she locked the door, leaving Mac-Dougal to whine unhappily on the other side of it. Then she realized she'd forgotten underwear, but she didn't dare go out again. Besides having to deal with the dog, she had Wyatt to consider. He could come in at any minute, and she wanted to be dressed when he invaded the house again.

Invasion was the only word she could think of in connection with Wyatt. He'd burst into her world with all the force of a rodeo bull coming out of the chute, and he'd caused more turmoil and confusion in a few hours than any man she'd ever encountered.

Every time she thought of his crude remark concerning chaps and a rope, she wanted to hit something. Or someone. A certain someone. When he'd touched her with his gloved hand it had merely reminded her of his heroic effort to rescue Alistair. That was absolutely all there was to it. She admired that sort of courage and resourcefulness. Instead of recognizing that, he'd turned her response into something distasteful, implying that she was some sort of bondage freak. Disgusting.

She'd wanted to lock the French doors against him, too, but he'd have found some way, perhaps a way that would damage the door, to get in. He wasn't the sort of man who would allow her to lock him out of the house on a freezing day. He was a very resolute character.

Determination was admirable in some contexts, Charity realized, and dangerous in others. The same persistent behavior that had saved Alistair could very well be her undoing unless she made it very clear she didn't want anything more to do with Wyatt. He was obviously highly sexed and unable to spend twenty-four hours in the company of an available woman without trying to seduce her. She mustn't allow that to happen.

Just as she finished combing her hair and fastening it on top of her head, she heard the French doors open. Taking a deep breath, she came out of the bathroom. "Hold it," she commanded, halting him in the open doorway. MacDougal greeted Wyatt as joyously as he had greeted her. The dog was a complete traitor. "I can't have you walking all through the house making a mess," she said.

"Want me to strip right here, then?"

She'd have to ignore remarks like that, she told herself, even if they did make her heart pound and her cheeks flush. "Yes. After I leave." She moved quickly to Nora's closet. "I think Nora has a bathrobe in here you can wear to get yourself decently back to your room." She quickly sorted through the garments hanging in the closet and found a blue satin robe—trimmed in white fur. Served him right. She pulled it from the hanger.

"This should work." She crossed the room toward him and laid the robe over a chair positioned next to the French doors.

He glanced at the robe, then back at her. "You picked that one on purpose, didn't you? Nora probably has a plaid flannel robe hanging right next to it."

"I really have no idea." She turned and headed out of the room. "But I'm sure you'll look lovely in that," she added over her shoulder. "Just dump your wet clothes in the bathtub." Then she called the dog, but

MacDougal didn't come. The turncoat had chosen to stay with Wyatt.

NORA'S BEDROOM window shade was up, but Alistair couldn't see anything incriminating going on in the bedroom except for Charity making free with Nora's clothes. The two women were about the same size. *Had been* about the same size, he reminded himself. It was so difficult to think of poor, dear Nora in the past tense. No doubt Charity planned on expanding her wardrobe now that Nora wouldn't be needing anything.

He watched Charity toss some blue silk garment on a chair. She was talking to someone. Alistair figured out that the nephew must be standing just inside the French doors. Then Charity left the room. The nephew hadn't come into view yet, but he would. If Alistair was lucky, the nephew might take this opportunity to go through Nora's jewelry chest.

Alistair slapped his forehead. His video camera! He nearly tripped going down the stairs to get it. Thank goodness he always kept it loaded. In less than a minute he was back, winded but ready to film. Gasping from his run up and down the stairs, he trained the viewfinder on the window.

He'd been prepared to watch the nephew poke through Nora's jewelry and pocket a few of her valuables. He'd hoped that would happen, so he could get it on film. He hadn't been prepared for the nephew to walk past the window wearing a woman's blue silk robe trimmed in white fur. Alistair nearly dropped the camera. The nephew was not only a murderer, he was a cross-dresser. And Alistair had the proof on film.

CHARITY LEFT Wyatt with the prospect of wearing the fur-trimmed robe and went downstairs to check on the fire. She was chilled to the bone, and the fire was the only source of heat in the house. Well, not the only source, but the safest one. Wyatt's kisses had made her forget the cold completely, but giving in to that temptation again would truly be playing with fire.

The coals smoldered, nearly out, and the room was much colder than it had been when she and Wyatt had left it earlier. Without electricity the fireplace really was their salvation, she realized, poking at the embers with one of Nora's decorative brass fireplace tools. She added more wood and blew on the coals to get the blaze going again.

"Why not use the bellows?" Wyatt asked from the doorway.

She turned and had to clamp her lips together to keep from hooting with laughter at the sight of him in Nora's blue silk. His broad shoulders strained the armhole seams. Instead of the cleavage that the robe was designed to reveal, a mat of dark hair was exposed where the white fur collar inadequately covered the muscled expanse of his chest. His strong calves, also sprinkled with dark hair, stood out in sharp contrast to the fur trimming the robe's hemline.

The quivering fur of the hemline was too much of a temptation for Mac. He made a grab for it, but Wyatt jumped out of the way just in time. "No!" he commanded, hiking the robe out of the dog's reach.

Charity would have given anything for a camera.

"There's a bellows hanging right there." Wyatt gestured with one flowing sleeve while he held the robe's hem away from the dancing dog with the other hand.

Charity nearly choked with the effort not to laugh. "I know," she said in a strained voice. "But they're antique."

"So use 'em anyway. Down, Mac."

Surprisingly, the little dog dropped to his belly.

Wyatt strode into the room, white fur trim flouncing. "You'll never get the fire going blowing on it that way."

"Wait," Charity protested around a giggle as she rose to her feet and placed a protective hand on the bellows. "Really. We can't use them. I don't think Nora's kept the leather oiled and it'll probably crack."

Wyatt glared at her, then down at the fire. A wisp of fur got near his mouth and he blew it away impatiently.

That did it. Charity doubled over in helpless laughter.

"You think this getup is real funny, don't you?" Wyatt challenged.

She looked at him through eyes streaming with tears. "Yes!"

"Would you like me to leave it on for the rest of the day, so you can be entertained?"

Still grinning, she took off her glasses and wiped her eyes on her sleeve. "That won't be necessary. The image of you in that robe is firmly planted in my brain."

He nodded. "You know, revenge can be a dangerous path to follow."

Something in his tone of voice warned her to be careful, yet she still held the upper hand, and she decided to make the most of it. She met his gaze. "Are you threatening me—" her lips trembled with suppressed laughter "—ma'am?" She knew from the flash in his dark eyes that perhaps she'd pushed him too far.

He pulled her roughly against him before she could step out of reach. "In my experience, revenge usually backfires," he said.

She struggled to free herself, belatedly realizing that her motions had loosened the slippery silk and she was pressed disturbingly close to a very naked, very aroused man. Liquid heat seared through her as Wyatt gazed into her eyes.

His voice was husky with desire. "I was prepared to forget what happened between us out on the balcony. But when you forced me to wear this robe, I decided it was a signal that you wanted to continue the fun and games."

"No," she protested, although her body was saying something completely different. "No, I just...."

"As I started to say before Updegraff interrupted us, it looks as if we'll be alone together for some time." His breath was a warm caress on her face. "You'd better decide what you want." Then he released her, retied the robe and left the room. A brief whistle brought Mac to his feet to follow him.

Charity stood trembling, not from the cold, which she'd forgotten entirely, but from the wave of sensuality that had washed over her as Wyatt held her tight in his arms. *Decide what you want.* Twenty-four hours ago she would have been able to. But ever since Wyatt had first touched her, she'd felt like a damaged compass with its directional needle whirling out of control.

She took a deep breath and knelt to take care of the dying fire. The effort of nursing it back to life helped calm her and redirect her thoughts to other practical matters. She and Wyatt had more important things to worry about than their sexual appetites. Feeding themselves, for one thing. She'd give a first edition of Dickens for a cup of coffee right now. Glancing at the cheerful fire, she wondered if there might be a way to brew some.

A tour of the house produced an enamelware coffeepot. Charity opened the back door long enough to scoop some snow into it. After ladling coffee grounds into the basket and making a silent apology to Nora, she used the fireplace tongs to nestle the pot in the midst of the flames. As she feared, black soot quickly coated the pot, but the heavenly scent of brewing coffee filling the room made up for it.

Just as she stood and turned to get a couple of coffee mugs from the kitchen, Wyatt appeared dressed in jeans. He was in the process of buttoning a clean Western-style shirt, and Mac trotted happily at his heels.

"Do I smell coffee?" Wyatt asked.

Charity's mouth went dry at the sight of his muscular chest. He sent shivers of desire through her without even trying. She cleared her throat and motioned back toward the fire. "I found a coffeepot."

He finished with the buttons, leaving the top two undone. "Must not be an antique, then." He walked toward her.

"I'm afraid it is."

His eyebrows lifted. "And you sacrificed it for our coffee? I'm impressed."

"I'll clean the pot before Nora comes back. And I should warn you, I have no idea how the coffee will taste. I've never done this before in my life."

"Just so it's hot and strong."

She wished he hadn't phrased it quite that way. Hot and strong was exactly how she'd describe him. She looked away from his dark gaze and walked past him.

"I'll get a couple of mugs and we can find out. I think there are some muffins in the bread box."

"I'll come with you. We'd better check the refrigerator to find out if we should put any of the food into a snowbank outside. And plan what we're going to eat today besides muffins."

Her heart raced just having him walk behind her into the kitchen. She'd have to get a grip. "I thought you wanted a complete turkey dinner?"

"You didn't seem to think that was an option."

She went to the cupboard to get the mugs. "Maybe we could put the covered roaster on the coals just like I did the coffeepot and keep the fire going around it." She took two mugs from the shelf and turned. "What do you think?"

He closed the refrigerator door. "That's a twenty-pound turkey in there. It would be damn near impossible to get the roaster in and out of the fire."

She'd wanted praise for her idea and instead he was throwing up obstacles. "Then I guess we'll have peanut butter sandwiches, won't we?"

"Now, don't get like that. I didn't say it couldn't be done."

She couldn't seem to erase the peevish tone from her voice. "Yes, you did. You—"

"Hey."

The soft syllable cut through her irritation. She stared at him for a long moment.

"Can I see what the turkey roaster looks like?" he asked.

She set the mugs on the counter and crouched to open a lower cupboard. While pulling the roaster out, she had time to think about her behavior, and concluded she'd overreacted. She stood and turned back to him, the roaster in her arms. "I'm sorry. This such a crazy situation, and I—"

"Yeah, I know," he said gently. He stepped forward and took the roaster from her unresisting grip.

She found herself staring at the open neck of his shirt and wondering how the swirl of chest hair she glimpsed there would feel beneath her fingertips. She looked up, and for one heart-stopping moment she thought he might kiss her again.

Instead he smiled and started out of the kitchen. "Let's go have some of that coffee while I think about the turkey roaster problem."

"D-do you want muffins?" she stammered.

"You bet," he called back to her. "I'm starving."

She put the muffins into a basket and grabbed an oven mitt, mugs and napkins before returning to the living room.

Wyatt sat cross-legged on the floor in front of the fire. With Mac stationed nearby, head cocked, Wyatt considered the turkey roaster on his lap. His duffel bag lay open beside him, which reminded her of his remark about chaps and a rope for making love. She'd hated that remark, yet perversely, just thinking of it made her weak with desire.

He glanced up, a smile of triumph on his face. "I reckon I've got it figured out."

"Really?" Her heart gave a little jump at the brilliance of that smile.

He pulled a coil of wire out of the duffel. "I'll twist strands of baling wire together, loop them through the handles and make the roaster into a basket with a lid. The wire handle will be high enough above the flames that I can reach in and grab hold of it without getting burned."

"You carry wire around with you? Whatever for?"

"Everything. Fixing tack, wiring a bumper back on my truck, making a turkey roaster handle. Most cowboys would be lost without a length of baling wire handy."

"Amazing." If she'd unconsciously classified him as a dumb cowboy, she'd been dead wrong. She recognized a creative mind at work.

He glanced at her. "Thanks." Then he set the roaster on the floor beside him and got to his feet. "Let's get that coffee poured."

"It's going to take two of us." She put down the basket of muffins and the mugs. "One to use the fireplace tongs and the other to grab the handle with the oven mitt."

"I'll handle the tongs."

She nodded and pulled on the oven mitt. The system worked like a charm. Wyatt snagged the pot from the front so the handle faced Charity. When she took hold of it, he put the tongs down and picked up the mugs. In moments she'd poured the coffee and they sat in front the fire. Charity sipped the coffee and sighed with pleasure.

"I second that," Wyatt said. "You brew a fine pot of coffee, lady."

She smiled at him. "Thanks."

"You're welcome." His gaze was warm and compelling.

An uneasy trembling began deep inside her. She could marshal arguments against the idea all day, but the truth was, she wanted to make love to him. And judging from the slow smile touching his lips, he knew it. Looking away from that knowing smile, she took a quick gulp of coffee and scalded her tongue.

8

THE COFFEE and muffins took the edge off Wyatt's hunger, but he was used to eating more hearty food. After a second cup of coffee, he set his mug on the hearth and glanced at Charity. "Let's get that bird in the roaster."

"Good idea." She dusted crumbs from her hands into the muffin basket.

He took note of the gesture, a nicety he hadn't bothered with. No question that she was more civilized than he was, which only added to the attraction... and the challenge. Her dusting motion also confirmed something he'd suspected when he'd held her during the blue bathrobe incident—she wasn't wearing a bra. It could be a feminist statement, of course, but then again, it could be intended as a more provocative kind of message. He sincerely hoped so. His fantasies of making love to her were becoming almost unmanageable.

Charity stood. "If you'll get the roaster ready, I'll go do... whatever needs to be done with the bird."

He chuckled as he reached for his duffel bag. "Okay. You know you have to take the guts out, right?"

"They're not already out?"

She sounded so distressed he took pity on her. "Yeah, but I'm pretty sure they wrap them in butcher paper or something and shove them back in."

"Now why would anyone do such a crazy thing?"

"Some people make gravy with them. I think my mom does." He glanced up. "Haven't you ever hung around the kitchen when your mom made Thanksgiving dinner?"

"When I was little I watched my brothers while she did it. And then—she quit." The change in her expression was subtle, a tightening around her mouth and a slight flare to her nostrils.

He kept his tone light, not wanting to frighten her away from the source of her anger. "How come?"

She gazed down at him and seemed to consider whether or not to answer. Finally she did. "My father left us for another woman the day after Thanksgiving."

Ah. He understood a lot more about her now. "That's terrible. I'm sorry, Charity."

"I'm not." Her chin lifted. "We were all better off without him, including my mother. What a jerk, stuffing himself on the food she'd worked so hard to prepare, when all along he planned to abandon us the next day."

"That's pretty cold."

She blinked and brought her glance back to his. "It taught me young what a trap marriage is for women."

"Sometimes it's a trap for men, too," he said quietly. He didn't condone what her father had done, but there were always two sides to any story.

"A trap for men, you say? Have you heard the latest statistics about high blood pressure? Married women's is higher than single women's. And for men, there's no difference whatsoever between husbands and bachelors. How about that?"

He shrugged. "I don't put much faith in statistics."

"Especially when they dispute your theories, right?"

He opened his mouth to fire another retort but stopped himself and lowered his head to stare at the baling wire in his hands. He didn't have the heart for this fight. After all, she'd been hurt at a young age by the one guy she'd trusted above all others. On the surface he could understand, but he didn't really know what that kind of betrayal was like. Right now he just wanted a way to douse the angry sparks they always seemed to strike off each other.

He glanced up and reached a hand toward her, palm up. "Please come back down here a minute."

Apprehension flickered in her eyes. "Why?"

"Because I have something I'd like to say to you and it'd be a whole lot easier if I didn't have to crane my neck like this."

Slowly she put her hand in his. Her touch stirred him more than he would have thought possible, but he kept control of himself. He guided her down until she knelt across from him.

"That's better." He looked into her blue eyes. "First of all, what your father did was rotten. Don't ever imagine that I approve of that kind of behavior. I believe in honoring commitments."

She swallowed. "That makes you an unusual man, then."

"You had a bad experience." He wanted to be gentle, but he wanted to make his point, too. "You're a smart woman, Charity. You know it's not logical to blame us all for what your father did."

Her gaze darkened. "Let's just say I have more than one example of the lies men tell women to get what they want."

He recognized a pattern he'd seen before—instinct sent her after men who were the spitting image of her father. Charity needed a steady lover, one who would stay. But Wyatt wasn't a stay-around kind of guy. Maybe that was his big attraction for her. If he cared about Charity at all he'd keep his distance. Somehow.

He released her hand and looked away from the challenge in her eyes. "Well, you don't have to worry about broken promises with me. I don't make them in the first place."

What appeared to be disappointment flickered on her face before she composed herself and stood. "At least you're honest. That's something."

"That's everything."

"Yes." She gave him a long look. "I guess it is." Then she turned and walked into the kitchen.

He had the insane urge to call her back. And beneath that was an even more dangerous compulsion, one that would mean the end of life as he knew it. He wanted to make her happy.

ALISTAIR WASN'T WILD about heights, but the occasion called for fearless behavior. He lifted the sash of the attic window and adjusted his muffler over the lower part of his face as the cold slapped his cheeks. The aluminum extension ladder clanked as he hoisted it to the sill and pushed it out the window about three feet. He wished Nora could be witness to the courage he was displaying in catching her killers. Perhaps she was watching from on high. Poor Nora.

Keeping his foot on the bottom rung of the ladder, Alistair extended it as far as it would go. Thank heaven the metal was lightweight, he thought, or he'd never have been able to lift the ladder and position it against

Nora's snowy roof. And thank heaven the houses were close together. Dear, departed Cordelia had complained about that, but the proximity was coming in handy now.

He settled the ladder firmly, made sure the small tape recorder and sturdy twine were safely in his pocket, and began the climb from the attic window to Nora's roof. He'd had the idea while stoking up the fire in his fireplace. Charity and the nephew were bound to their fireplace as much as he was to his. All he had to do was climb to their roof, lower the recorder down the chimney and collect that evil pair's secrets on tape. He would be silent and stealthy as a panther, clever as a fox, lightfingered as a raccoon. They'd never even suspect he was there.

CHARITY STUDIED the directions on the turkey wrapper before peeling it off and plopping the turkey in the sink. Sure enough, Wyatt had been right about obnoxious-looking turkey parts hidden inside the bird. There was no butcher paper wrapping, however.

But then, Wyatt was the man who made no promises, not even about butcher paper. That should make anything that happened between them easier, Charity reasoned. She had no intention of tying herself to a man and he had no intention of tying himself to a woman. They could have the sort of uncomplicated sex she'd always thought would be so liberating. So why did she feel as if an elephant's foot was planted on her chest every time she thought about a one-night stand with Wyatt?

"This is beginning to look like the set of 'E.R.,' " he commented from the kitchen doorway. He held the roaster by its baling wire handle.

She glanced at the drainboard where she'd been flinging whatever she found inside the turkey, and had to admit she'd made a gruesome mess. "Your mother uses this glop in gravy?"

"Let's not."

"Yeah, let's not." She eyed the turkey. "Do you think we should stuff it?"

"I'll take a wild guess. No, we shouldn't stuff it."

"Right answer. But the directions say to rinse it, and the water's off."

"I'll melt snow in the roaster." He opened the back door just long enough to scoop the snow. As he closed it again, a clank came from somewhere outside.

"What was that?" Charity asked.

"Heck if I know. Maybe something settling." Wyatt headed down the hall, Mac trotting at his heels. "I'll go heat this on the fire."

Charity wiped her hands on a paper towel and found a plastic bag for the turkey parts. She dumped the bag in the garbage pail just as Wyatt returned with the melted snow.

"Snow settling doesn't sound like metal clanking," she said to him as she lifted the turkey into the water.

"I wouldn't know. I'm an Arizona boy."

Charity glanced up at him. "It was a distinctive clank, sort of hollow, like one of those extension ladders banging against something."

"A ladder? In this weather?"

"You don't suppose that Alistair..."

"After the snowshoe incident?" Wyatt grinned. "He's probably so embarrassed he'll go into hiding until spring."

The snowshoe incident. When Wyatt had first kissed her. She looked away from the temptation of his smile.

"You don't know Alistair or you wouldn't say that."
She tried to get her hands under the slippery turkey to
turn it over but she kept losing her grip.

Wyatt stepped closer. "Here, let me help with that."
He shoved his hands under the turkey. "On three. One,
two—"

Charity remembered that the last time they'd counted
to three they'd ended up in each other's arms. "Wait,
I—"

"Three."

He lifted, but she didn't. Twenty pounds of unbal-
anced turkey flipped over toward them, tipping the
roaster and sending water splashing down the front of
her sweat suit and Wyatt's shirt.

The turkey tumbled out of the roaster and would
have hit the floor if Wyatt hadn't made a dive and
caught it in both arms.

They stared at each other for a moment in shock.

Charity recovered first. "Good catch."

"Star receiver in high school." With a nonchalance
that impressed her, considering he must be as cold and
wet as she was, he deposited the turkey back in the
roaster. "Bird's rinsed."

"I do believe it is."

He gave her a crooked grin. "Let's put the heat to this
baby."

Her heart somersaulted. Oh, he had a way about him,
this Wyatt Logan. "Anything you say." She followed
him into the living room and wondered if he guessed
how literally she'd meant that last statement.

Wyatt put the lid on the roaster and lifted the whole
thing by the baling wire. "Take the poker and adjust the
wood underneath as I let it down so it'll lie easy."

"Sure thing." She picked up the brass poker, once polished and pristine but now blackened with soot, and began rearranging the wood chunks to make a hotbed for the roaster. "You know, I think this is going to work."

"Of course it is. We're a good team." Wyatt hunkered down beside her and lifted the roaster over the low flames. His shoulder muscles bunched beneath the damp shirt as he slowly lowered the roaster.

"If you don't count a few minor disasters."

Wyatt let the weight of the roaster settle into the wood, made one more adjustment and pulled back from the fire. "Can't make an omelette without breaking a few eggs." He glanced at her. "By the way, how'd you dispose of the guts?"

"Plastic bag in the garbage."

"We should probably put them out in the snow before they start to stink."

Charity shuddered. "I definitely didn't like that part. It reminded me that we have a victim here."

"Well, I was raised on a ranch, so I'll put the guts out in the snow."

"I'll do it. I need to toughen up. No use being a hypocrite about it. After all, I'm going to enjoy—" She was cut off by Mac's furious barking, followed by something landing with a clank on top of the roaster lid.

"What in hell?" Wyatt grabbed the tongs and dragged out a slightly melted tape recorder attached to a piece of twine that was still smoking.

Mac kept barking.

"Hush!" Charity ordered, grabbing the little dog as she strained to hear above his frantic yapping. "Wyatt, listen! Someone's up there!"

Still holding the tape recorder with the tongs, Wyatt peered at it, then gazed toward the fireplace where hollow scraping sounds, coughing and what might have been muffled curses echoed down the chimney. Wyatt spoke in a low voice. "And it's too early for Santa Claus. This neighbor is getting weird, Charity."

"Tell me about it," she murmured.

"I wonder how in hell he got up there."

"I can't imagine."

"Maybe he's totally flipped out. People can do amazing things when they're crazy."

"I think we should try talking to him."

"Okay. Since you have a stake in this, let me try. Then he can get mad at me if I push the wrong buttons." Laying the recorder on the hearth, Wyatt moved over to the fireplace and called up the chimney. "Hey, Updegraff, whatcha doing on the roof, buddy?"

There was a long silence. Finally the answer drifted down the chimney. "Ice dams. Checking to see if you have any in the gutters. Can ruin a roof, you know."

Wyatt turned a questioning glance toward Charity, who shrugged in response. Wyatt leaned toward the opening again. "That's right neighborly of you, Updegraff. But you'll have to excuse me, 'cause I'm just an old cowpoke from Arizona and I don't know how y'all do things here in the East. How does the, uh, tape recorder fit into that project?"

More silence. Then another answer came through the chimney. "Found it and thought you might want to use it for music, or something. Runs on batteries."

Wyatt gazed at the melted recorder. "Not anymore. Did you happen to notice we had a fire going here?"

"Of course I noticed!" Alistair's temper flared. "What do you take me for, an idiot?"

"Well, now, that's not an easy question to answer, buddy."

"I am *not* your buddy. I can see my efforts are not appreciated, so I'll just leave you to worry about your own ice dams. I'm going home."

"How're you getting there?" Wyatt asked casually.

"Same way I got over here."

Wyatt glanced at Charity.

"The ladder!" she whispered. "I'll bet he extended it between the two houses!"

"The old guy could kill himself crawling back."

Charity leapt up. "Maybe we can see from Nora's bedroom. Maybe we can talk him across, like you see in the movies."

"I'm beginning to think this *is* a movie. Let's go."

They raced up the stairs with Mac in hot pursuit, barking all the way. When they reached Nora's bedroom they crowded together at the window and peered upward at the ladder stretched between the houses. Alistair was balanced on the rungs, inching his way backward toward his attic window.

"I'll be damned," Wyatt said. "I wouldn't have thought Updegraff had the *cajones* to try something like that."

"Cajones?"

"That's Spanish for balls."

"Oh." Charity didn't need the added stimulation of that remark while she was standing hip-to-hip with a man who had more *cajones* than any guy she'd ever known. She should be thinking of poor Alistair, who seemed to be several bricks shy of a load. She should be too distraught to notice the wonderful friction between denim and pink cotton. "Do you think we should say anything to him?" she whispered.

Wyatt's chest heaved in a massive sigh. "Probably not. If we let him know we're here watching, it might distract him. But at least we're here if he does fall. We can do...something."

"What on earth could we do?"

"I don't know. I'd lower myself down with a rope, maybe. We'd figure it out."

Charity felt a rush of confidence, knowing that she and Wyatt would figure it out and Alistair would have the best help anyone could expect under very difficult circumstances. "We need to notify somebody," she said. "He's become a danger to himself."

Wyatt glanced down at her. "And how are you planning to do that? Smoke signals?"

She saw his point. All three of them were cut off from the outside world, at least for the next few hours. And Nora's neighbor had chosen this inopportune time to go bonkers. "But what if he tries this routine again? He might make it once, but I can't believe he'd be lucky twice."

"Once he's inside, we could knock the ladder down before he has a chance to pull it back."

"Brilliant!" Charity started for the door. "You keep watch and I'll get a broom."

"Hurry."

"I was a star sprinter in high school."

She raced back downstairs, nearly tripping over MacDougal as he bounced along beside her, obviously certain this was a game. Yanking open the pantry door, she grabbed the broom and ran back upstairs. She was panting by the time she returned. "Am I too late?"

"Just in time. He's almost inside." Without looking at her, he pushed up the window and held out his hand for the broom.

She gave it to him. Unable to turn away from the unfolding drama, she stood in the cold draft of the open window and hugged herself against the frigid feel of damp, chilled cotton against her breasts and belly. Alistair lowered his butt to get it under the window frame.

"Now," Charity urged in a breathless whisper. "Do it right *now.*"

"I love it when you talk dirty." With a grunt of effort Wyatt swung the broom handle against the ladder just as Alistair glanced over at them.

"You fiends!" the little man screamed, grabbing for the ladder. But he wasn't quick enough. With a solid thump the ladder landed far below him and submerged itself in the snow, leaving a perfect imprint where it fell.

"You did it!" Charity knocked the broom out the window as she hugged him enthusiastically.

"*We* did it." He smiled down at her as he wrapped her in his arms. "Track star."

"I'll get you yet!" Alistair cried. "You haven't seen the last of Alistair Updegraff!"

"We can always hope," Wyatt said. Keeping one arm around Charity, Wyatt pushed the window closed and pulled down the shade. Then he carefully took off Charity's glasses. And then he kissed her.

9

HE SHOULDN'T be doing this, Wyatt thought as he lost himself in the sweet coffee and muffin taste of Charity's mouth. Less than an hour ago he'd decided she needed somebody else, anybody else. But logic had failed him when she'd come so eagerly into his arms.

She was so delicious he couldn't seem to get enough of her. He kept changing the angle of the kiss to delve deeper, and she responded. Lord, how she responded. She'd been breathless from her run up the stairs, but now she was gasping with a different rhythm entirely as she pulled his head down and whimpered against his mouth.

He tossed her glasses over on Nora's bed so he could have the use of both hands. First he released her hair from its confinement and splayed his fingers through the silky mass as he kissed her lips, her chin, her nose, her flushed cheeks.

"I . . . lied about . . . being a track star," she gasped.

"Did you?" He thrust his tongue deep into her mouth, not caring at the moment if she was a serial killer. He slipped both hands beneath her sweatshirt and slid them up the smooth warmth of her back.

She screeched.

He leapt back as if she'd slapped him. "What? What's wrong?"

"Your hands are *freezing*."

"Oh." He looked down at his hands. "Sorry." Gradually the haze of passion that had made him a self-centered bundle of testosterone receded.

She stepped toward him. "Let me warm them up. I—"

"Listen, I think we need to talk."

"Talk?" She looked bewildered and a little hurt. "But you said I should decide what I wanted. I've decided, Wyatt, in case you couldn't tell."

He vaguely remembered saying something like that, but that was before she'd spilled her guts about her history with men, beginning with her father. "I guess I'm a little worried about your reasons for deciding we should make love, that's all."

Hurt gave way to indignation. "We're back to that? You think I have some plan to snare you into marriage? Well, you can take that attitude and shove it right up your—"

"No." He closed the gap between them and took her by the arms. "I don't think that at all. I think you expect me to leave."

"And the sooner the better. Who needs you?"

"Look, we're both still wet, and we have to keep that fire going downstairs. Let's get into some dry clothes and continue this discussion where it's warmer."

She shook herself out of his grip. "You can discuss all you want. I'm through with this little game. I wouldn't make love to you if you were the last man on earth."

If he left it at that, with Charity furious, he'd accomplish his goal of not breaking her heart. Anger was a good shield for her, and besides, he was no shrink. If he tried to explain why he wasn't good for her she'd probably resent the hell out of being psychoanalyzed. He would if somebody tried to do that to him. Not that he needed it. He knew exactly what he wanted and where he was going. Of course he did.

She squinted up at him. "Do you *have* any dry clothes?"

He noticed the squint and walked to the bed to retrieve her glasses. "Come to think of it, no, I don't." He handed her the glasses.

"You notice these aren't rose-colored," she said as she put them on.

"I never thought they were."

"I know perfectly well that you're a traveling rodeo man. I would have been perfectly able to handle the conditions of our short relationship."

"Maybe you're right about not discussing this. We'll only get tangled up in an argument again."

"We're already tangled up in an argument. And you started it."

"Now, that's not fair. I'm only—"

Mac whined, for the first time making his presence known since the window had closed.

Wyatt glanced over at the dog sitting beside the bed, his head cocked to one side as if trying to figure out what the problem was. "I don't think he likes it when we fight," Wyatt said.

"I'm sure he doesn't." She swung abruptly away from him and stomped over to a double dresser. "It's touching how concerned you are about the dog's feelings." Wrenching open a drawer, she flipped through the garments stacked there before slamming the drawer and opening the next one. "By all means, let's be careful about the dog's feelings. Let's not make things difficult for the *dog,* for heaven's sake." She pulled a garment from the drawer and threw it at him. "Take that downstairs and put it on. And take the dog." Her voice caught. "I'm sure you'll take good care of him."

"Dammit, Charity, I care about your feelings!"

"Sure you do! That's why you announce you're not interested, then change your mind, then change your mind again!" Her eyes filled with tears. "All of that shilly-shallying around is probably to save my feelings, isn't it?"

"In a way, yes."

"Then *stop* thinking about my feelings. Because you're making a complete mess of things."

She had a point. He hadn't bungled an encounter with a woman since eighth grade, and even that hadn't been this bad. "See you downstairs," he said as he left the room.

At least she hadn't given him another fur-trimmed silk bathrobe, he thought as he unbuttoned his clammy shirt on the trip down the stairs. The deep blue sweatshirt with orange lettering was from Aunt Nora's alma mater, Syracuse University. It was softened from years of washing and seemed way too big to have belonged to Nora.

Wyatt hung his shirt over the back of the sofa and pulled the sweatshirt over his head. Then he went to work on the fire under the turkey roaster. The room had already begun to fill with the aroma of cooking turkey, and the scent prompted inconvenient memories of cozy holiday dinners and laughter around a family table. But his parents were getting older. Aunt Nora was getting older. Eventually Wyatt would face holidays alone. He'd never contemplated where his carefree existence would eventually take him. He didn't want to contemplate it now, either. If he wasn't careful about this sentimental stuff, he'd wind up doing something really stupid this weekend.

ALISTAIR HUDDLED in front of his brick fireplace, an afghan around his shoulders while he sipped some bracing Earl Grey. Desperate for the consolation of tea, he'd used a coat hanger to dangle a saucepan over the fire until the water became reasonably hot. He'd never liked scalding tea, anyway. He'd covered the bottom of the pan with aluminum foil to prevent soot from blackening its exterior.

The Earl Grey helped him get over the shock of the past hour. He'd known he was dealing with cold-hearted criminals, but he hadn't imagined the depth of their depravity. This was a true crime novel in the making if he'd ever seen one.

His tape recorder plan had been working splendidly, until the conversation below filtered up to him. Horrified yet fascinated, he'd leaned over the chimney to hear better. And what he heard! They'd disemboweled Nora and put her entrails in a plastic bag! But a puff of smoke had made him start to choke, and he'd dropped the string holding the recorder.

At least he'd learned that they planned to freeze the entrails in the snow outside. He had to find that plastic bag and save the gory evidence for the authorities. A modern autopsy lab would be able to identify the entrails as Nora's, and Alistair would testify who had put the bag there in the first place. Alistair shuddered to think what they'd done with the rest of the body. Maybe they hoped to dispose of it piece by piece. After all, they had been sawing in the laundry room the night before. Diabolical schemers.

He had but one avenue left. He wasn't the physical specimen he'd once been, but whatever strength he had would have to suffice. The effort might temporarily cripple him, but it was a necessary sacrifice. He had to tunnel over.

SHIVERING from cold and smarting from Wyatt's rejection, Charity flung the damp pink sweat suit into the tub with the other wet clothes and found a white one. She also took the time to borrow some underwear she came across in a bag in Nora's drawer, the tags still attached, and was surprised at the seductive quality of it. Apparently Nora's practical clothing had hidden a secret desire for feminine frills.

Nora's bras were all the underwire type, which Charity had previously disdained because she'd always thought they were designed by a man with a breast fetish. An underwire bra was better than none, she reasoned, but after putting it on, she wasn't so sure. The construction emphasized her bustline and gave her some impressive cleavage. Of course, no one would be able to see that as long as her sweatshirt remained on. And it would.

The panties were cut high on her thigh and banded with peek-a-boo lace. Charity had never owned such sexy underthings, and wearing them had the disturbing effect of reminding her of the pleasures to be provided by a man's hands and a man's mouth. And not just any man, either. The one waiting for her downstairs. Her womb tightened in response to that thought.

But Wyatt believed she was the bait in a matrimonial trap set for him, and as long as he believed that, pride would keep her from making a fool of herself, no matter what type of underwear she wore.

She fastened her hair on top of her head, took a deep breath, and started downstairs. Partway down she could smell the turkey roasting and suddenly she realized how hungry she'd become. The turkey wouldn't be done for quite a while, so she and Wyatt needed to find something to snack on. That would take up time and energy for both of them, which was a good thing.

At the foot of the stairs she paused and glanced into the living room. The sight that greeted her made her former anger at him disappear, and she clutched the newel post while she stared in speechless admiration. Wyatt, shirtless, his skin glistening with a sheen of perspiration, was doing push-ups in front of the fireplace.

Charity swallowed but didn't look away. She should have. The smooth precision of Wyatt's movements and the bulge of his considerable muscle mass made her knees wobble and her heart race. And the position itself reminded her so much of a different activity in which Wyatt's movements might be similar. She was in deep, deep trouble.

Wyatt finished the exercise and pushed himself to his feet. Then he turned and caught her staring at him. "I have a set of exercises I have to do every day to keep in shape for bull riding," he said, reaching for a towel he'd thrown over the arm of the rocker. He wiped the sweat from his face and draped the towel around his neck.

"Don't—" Charity stopped and cleared her throat. "Don't let me interrupt. I was just going in the kitchen to find us something to eat."

"Great idea. Smelling this turkey cooking is making me hungry."

Appetite. Wyatt seemed to have a healthy one in all respects, Charity thought as she hurried down the hall toward the kitchen. He appreciated food, laughter, exercise... and sex. After living most of her life immersed in intellectual pursuits, Charity hadn't thought much about her physical appetites. Now it seemed to be all she could think of.

In a few minutes she returned to the living room with a tray containing cheese, crackers, apples and a jar of cashews. MacDougal was asleep in his basket by the fire, and Wyatt, still bare-chested except for the towel draped around his neck, was shaving with a straight razor.

Charity stood transfixed by the scene, which could have been lifted right out of the seventeenth century. Wyatt sat on a chair positioned in front of an end table, where he'd propped a hand mirror and a decorative antique washbasin from the guest bedroom. The tangy scent of shaving cream wafted toward her, and she knew the fragrance would always be linked in her mind with Wyatt performing this masculine ritual.

His deft motions as he dragged the razor across his cheek and flicked the shaving cream into the basin indicated he was used to this method. Charity wasn't, and she watched in fascination, the tray forgotten in her hands.

"I'm also an expert with legs, if you're ever interested." He spoke without interrupting the steady rhythm of his task.

She'd been caught staring again, probably in the mirror he was using. Embarrassed, she set the tray on the coffee table with more than necessary clatter. "Isn't that special."

"So I've been told."

"I can't imagine why you're bothering to shave." Actually she could imagine, and the reason made her blood race through her veins. But of course he didn't want to risk being trapped.

He finished and wiped the last bits of shaving cream away with the towel before standing and turning toward her. "Habit," he said, tossing the towel aside and reaching for his discarded sweatshirt. He pulled it over his head, eliminating Charity's view of his muscled chest. "Guess we'd better check the bird."

"Guess so." She'd give anything for some of his nonchalance. There was a breathless quality to her voice that made her wince.

Fortunately he didn't seem to notice as he concentrated on lifting the roaster from the fire and setting it on the hearth. Using an oven mitt, he lifted the lid.

Charity walked over and peered under the lid. "Still looks pretty white."

"It's not done, but it sure smells great."

"Yes. Great." She was too overwhelmed by the scent of freshly shaven masculinity to notice.

He replaced the lid and stood. "I need to get some more wood from the garage and build up the fire before I put the roaster back on."

"How's the wood supply holding out?"

"We should have enough to last through tomorrow. After that I don't know what we'll do."

"I'm sure the power will be on again by then," Charity said, although she had no idea if it would be or not.

"Hope so. Be right back." He paused by the tray. "Looks perfect except we need a bottle of wine. I'll get it when I bring the wood."

She wasn't sure how he'd manage that, but she decided to wait and see rather than offer to help. After he left, she walked over and rubbed a clean place on the bay window glass to look outside. The view was unchanged from early that morning. Nothing moved in the frozen landscape except the occasional flutter of a bird.

It didn't look as if the power would come on anytime soon, which meant she would be spending the night alone here with Wyatt as he'd predicted. The logical plan would be for both of them to sleep by the fire. In fact, they should drag out the mattress from the guest room and set up camp in the living room for the night. The ever-present curl of tension deep within her turned a notch tighter.

Wyatt reappeared with a stack of wood and a bottle of red wine balanced vertically on top.

Charity stared at him in horror. "Wyatt! That bottle could fall and break!"

"What?" He grinned and pretended to stagger toward her.

"Stop clowning around! Red wine on that Sultanabad would be a disaster."

"The whosit? I don't see any sultans in here."

"The Sultanabad rug. I already told you it's a hundred and twenty years old."

"And how old's the wine?" He staggered again on his way to the fireplace. "Whoops!"

"Give me that bottle." She grabbed it off the top of the pile as he began to chuckle. "I suppose a good laugh is more important than a precious antique to you."

He deposited the wood on the hearth and starting laying a few pieces on the coals. "Matter of fact, it is." As he leaned toward the fireplace the back of his sweatshirt rode up, revealing two slender wineglasses, their stems shoved through his belt loops.

"Nora's crystal!" Charity cried, starting forward.

"Don't touch them," he ordered. "Let me handle this and nothing will break."

She held her breath as he finished with the fire, replaced the roaster and stood.

Then he gently pried the wineglasses loose and held them up for her inspection. "See? No problem."

"You were lucky. Crystal like that is so delicate. It can snap if you breathe on it wrong."

"I know. To be honest, this was a stunt to prove something to you. The last time I was in this house I was fifteen, and I was as clumsy as most fifteen-year-olds. That's what Aunt Nora remembers and what she's probably told you about me. But clumsy guys don't make it on the pro rodeo circuit, Charity." Then he tossed both glasses in the air.

"My God! You—" Her throat closed on the rest of the sentence as he began to juggle the goblets in a lazy rhythm. "You're insane," she whispered.

He caught the goblets and set them on the coffee table. "I'll admit to that. You have to be a little crazy to last on the circuit. But I'm not clumsy, Charity. So relax." He pulled a corkscrew from his front pocket, picked up the bottle and expertly removed the cork. "And have some wine," he added, pouring her a glass without spilling a drop.

"I can't take this." She sank to the sofa.

"Sure you can." He handed her the glass and picked up the second one for himself. "You've coped with every crisis we've had so far, and we've had a few." He finished pouring and raised his glass. "Here's to you, Charity. You're one hell of a woman."

"Don't do that."

"What?"

"You know." She took a steadying sip of wine. "Pay me compliments. Start everything up again."

He gazed at her. "You deserve the compliments, but I'll do my damnedest not to start anything I can't finish, much as I'd like to."

The wineglass trembled in her hand. "You... would?"

"Of course I would. Any man would be crazy not to want you. But for once in my life, I've decided to think about somebody besides myself. From what you've said, the last thing in the world you need is another love 'em and leave 'em type." He tasted his wine. "Which is exactly what I am."

Her jaw tensed. "I told you I wasn't interested in a permanent relationship."

"Why not?"

The tension moved to her temples, which began to throb. She swallowed more wine. "I value my freedom."

"To do what?"

He was deliberately trying to trick her, she decided, and make her reveal her domestic instincts. She drank her wine and took some time before answering. "Freedom to keep my own schedule, eat when I want, sleep when I want, work as late as I want."

He topped off her glass. "If you find the right guy, none of that would be a problem. Charity, you own a business, which means you're already tied down. Marriage might even give you more freedom because you'd have someone to share the burden of that business if you got sick, or wanted to take a trip. You've created a bogeyman when there isn't one. Marriage would be wonderful for you."

"How dare you presume to say that!"

"Because I have nothing to lose by telling you the truth. I can picture you in a home, playing with your children. You'd make a terrific mother."

"You are so wrong. I have no desire for children." The statement rang false to her, but she wouldn't give him the satisfaction of knowing that. "Absolutely no desire." She met his assessing gaze for as long as she could and finally used the excuse of sipping her wine to look away. "You don't know what you're talking about."

"Maybe not. But you wanted to know why I'd decided we shouldn't make love. That's it."

"How self-sacrificing." Anger and disappointment smoldered within her.

"Okay, so it's a little out of character."

She took another sip of her wine. Dutch courage, they called it, and she could see why. She was definitely feeling bolder now than when she'd first sat on the sofa after the juggling scene. "You know what I think?"

"I have a feeling I'm about to find out."

She pointed a finger at him. "You're scared. And that's why you won't make love to me."

"Scared? Now wait a minute. I—"

"You've been scared from the minute you found out Nora had asked me to stay and cook dinner for you. You thought it was a trap then, and you think it's a trap now. What's more, you're afraid you might get caught this time, because I believe you really do want me." She gained momentum as she talked, and discovered she didn't need the rest of her wine, after all. The goblet made an audible click as she set it on the coffee table. "Wanting me makes you vulnerable, doesn't it?"

His eyes darkened and he took a step forward. "Charity, so help me..."

"Help you what? I've told you I'm not interested in marriage, but you won't listen." She stood and braced her hands on her hips. The movement caused her sexy underwear to glide sensuously against her skin. "I think the person who couldn't handle an uncomplicated sexual relationship is you."

"I've walked away a hundred times. Once more is no problem."

Heart thudding, Charity lifted her chin. "Prove it."

He backed up at that. "Oh, no, you don't."

"See?" She stalked him. "You're petrified of me. I'm too much woman for you."

"That's a laugh." He'd reached the window seat by the bay window. He could retreat no further.

"You're not laughing. You're running." She paused and unfastened the pins from her hair. "I dare you to put down your wineglass."

"You don't know what you're doing. You're just repeating a familiar pattern."

"Not true. I've never seduced a rodeo man before." She took off her glasses and twirled them in one hand. Her vision was fuzzy now, but she didn't need a clear outline for this. In fact, blurry was better. It helped make her brave. Brave enough to take what she wanted.

"You know what I mean, Charity." He sounded a little desperate, a little frantic, and a lot worried. "You're only attracted to me because you know I'll leave you."

"What a convenient diagnosis, Dr. Freud." She laid the glasses on a nearby table and took a step closer. "Let's lie on your couch and discuss it, shall we?"

"Stop it." It was more of a plea than an order.

She chuckled low in her throat. "But I've only just started." She grasped the bottom of her sweatshirt and pulled the garment over her head. As he gasped, she praised the effects of underwire. Then she shook her hair. She couldn't see his expression, but he stooped down, and she heard the clunk of the wineglass as he set it beside him on the polished floor. Then he slowly straightened.

Her heartbeat thundered in her ears as she smiled and walked over to him. He was breathing hard. She tilted her face upward. "Have a little Charity, cowboy."

10

WYATT'S GROAN of surrender flowed over Charity, making her heady with triumph. Then he swept her into his arms with such force that her breath caught in her throat.

"Don't say I didn't try to do the right thing," he muttered before his lips descended to crush hers.

With that demanding kiss, he stripped away any remaining restraint between them. She wound both arms around his neck, arched against him and kissed him back with a seething desire no one else had guessed lay deep in her soul.

But Wyatt had guessed. As he tumbled her to the cushions of the window seat he seemed to know just where to touch, where to leave a lingering caress to bring out the wild, lusty spirit that Charity kept hidden from the world. A quick flick of his finger and the bra dropped away from her breasts. A swift tug with one hand and both her sweatpants and panties lay in a heap on the floor.

Charity reached for the hem of his sweatshirt, but he caught her wrists. "Wait."

"I want to feel you against me."

"You will." His mouth feathered kisses on hers, then moved lower to her throat. "Oh, you will," he murmured. "You'll feel me against you, within you, sur-

rounding you." He stretched her arms above her head
and leaned down to slowly draw one nipple into his
mouth.

She squirmed as the languorous tug reached from her
breast to her womb as if connected by a filament too
delicate to see yet too strong to break. She arched her
back as the filament tightened in response to his persistent caress. In answer he smoothed a hand over her
flat belly and spread his fingers when he encountered
the tangle of blond curls between her trembling thighs.
A teasing hesitation, and then he tunneled down to
claim her moist bounty with a deftness that left her
writhing in pleasure.

She couldn't control the plea that came to her lips as
he coaxed her closer to the brink of mindlessness. She
wanted more, asked for more, begged for more.

He released her breast and placed his lips close to her
ear. "Tell me exactly what you want." His whisper was
hoarse with urgency. "Tell me what you've never told
another man."

"I—" She hesitated.

"Tell me!" He raked his teeth across her earlobe and
pressed deep with his fingers against her throbbing
center.

And she did. Gasping with desire, she abandoned
shame in favor of gaining paradise. And he followed her
instructions in tender detail, sliding a pillow beneath her
hips as he kissed his way down the valley between her
ribs, stroking her thighs until they quivered beneath his
kneading fingers. At last he settled his clever mouth
against the most intimate part of her and loved her with
a thoroughness that made her helpless in his arms. Time
and again he took her to the edge before pulling back
until her breathing slowed. Then he'd begin the assault

again. She was sure she'd die of the exquisite torture
and willingly accepted her fate. But still she needed
more than this.

"I...want you inside me," she said, her voice ragged. "Please." Vaguely she knew that there was another step—some sort of protection was needed—but
she was too crazy with desire to care.

Wordlessly he returned to her side and pulled off his
sweatshirt. Then he unfastened his jeans. He held her
gaze as he shoved both jeans and briefs away and placed
her hand over his rigid shaft. "Is that what you want?"

She caressed him and he closed his eyes. "Yes. Do
you want to..." she said softly.

"Yes." He sucked in his breath. "I want this more
than I ever..."

She didn't ask him to finish the sentence. Nothing
mattered but the velvet skin beneath her fingers and the
thrusting evidence of his need. The ache within her became unbearable. "Come to me," she urged.

"Soon." He fumbled with his discarded jeans and
produced something from the pocket.

Briefly she wondered why a man who hadn't planned
to make love would carry a condom in his jeans' pocket,
but the question evaporated once he'd sheathed himself and moved over her.

"Can you see me?" he murmured as the tip of his
erection eased between the petals of her femininity.

"Come closer."

"My pleasure." He drove deep, his chest brushing the
tips of her breasts. "Close enough?"

She couldn't speak as she gazed into his eyes, dark
with the intensity of arousal. The knowledge that she
was completely joined with him at last robbed her of
words. She'd never felt such overwhelming needs, nor

such confidence that the man in her arms was the only one capable of filling them.

"Your eyes tell me yes."

She hadn't realized how precious that word could be. Wyatt pulled back and pushed forward again, and her mind echoed *yes*. He rocked again, and once again her body responded with a resounding *yes*. The affirmation pounded through her with each motion of his hips, each reconnection, each electric fusing of their bodies. Yes, yes, yes, *yes!*

The rhythm took them, obscuring the roles of who would lead, who would follow. The current swept them onward into a white water of raging passion, buffeting them mercilessly before hurling them, spent and gasping, over the tumbling, roaring cascade of release.

THROUGH A PEACEFUL HAZE of incredible satisfaction, the most satisfaction he could ever remember after making love, Wyatt gradually became aware of the sound of lapping. He opened one eye and leaned over the window seat to identify the sound.

MacDougal had finished Wyatt's wine, miraculously without dumping the glass over, and now had both paws on the coffee table while he attempted to get the last of Charity's wine. Before Wyatt had time to consider the consequences, he yelled at the dog.

MacDougal leapt away from the table, tipping it on end just as Charity struggled out from under Wyatt and pushed herself to a sitting position. Reflexively Wyatt covered her eyes with one hand while he watched the purple contents of the glass sail gracefully over a sizeable area of the ivory and pink surface of the Sultanabad rug. The moment seemed to last forever. Then

Wyatt's hope for a reprieve shattered as completely as the goblet when the antique crystal hit the floor.

Charity pulled his hand away from her eyes. "I heard crystal break!"

"A goblet."

She fumbled her way toward the edge of the window seat. "My glasses. Let me get my—"

"Hold it." He grabbed her by the waist. "There's another—"

But her swinging foot had already made contact with the second goblet, kicking it like a soccer ball. It, too, crashed with the distinctive tinkle of fine stemware breaking. "That was your wineglass," she whispered.

"Afraid so. Just stay here." Wyatt surveyed the room and found MacDougal in a corner looking owlishly at him.

As Wyatt considered whether to risk giving the Scottie a command or just going over and picking him up, the dog's hindquarters seemed to slide out from under him and slip sideways. Usually pert and upright, MacDougal lounged casually on the pine floor. He looked for all the world like a cowboy relaxing at his favorite honky-tonk.

Watching for glass beneath his feet, Wyatt crawled off the window seat. "Mac's plastered."

"Oh, *no.*"

"Guess it doesn't take much when you only weigh twenty pounds. I'd better lock him in the bathroom while I clean up the glass."

"Oh, Wyatt." She sounded totally dejected.

He grabbed an afghan from the window seat and draped it around her shoulders. "Hang on." He gave her a quick hug. "I'll be right back. And don't step down. There's glass right under your feet."

Without Charity's warmth or the heat wave of passion to keep him warm, Wyatt shivered as he stepped carefully around broken glass and made his way over to the dog. "It's okay, buddy." He crouched in front of the little dog. "Sorry I yelled at you. It wasn't your fault. We forgot you're a wino."

MacDougal looked at him with total nonchalance. Then he hiccuped.

"This is definitely a first," Wyatt muttered. "Come on, Mac. It's the drunk tank for you. Just—"

In a surprise move, the Scottie lunged to his feet and trotted unsteadily to a spot about ten feet away.

"Hey." Wyatt was amazed at how fast the little dog could move, considering he was blitzed. Or maybe Wyatt moved slower without the security of clothes. Truth to tell, he was freezing his butt off, not to mention other parts of his anatomy. He tried to stop shivering as he approached Mac with caution. He could swear the Scottie was laughing at him.

"I guess the wine's making him playful," Charity said.

"G-guess so," Wyatt said, trying to keep his teeth from chattering.

"You're getting cold. Why don't you—"

"I have to g-get him before he steps on that glass." Wyatt lowered his voice as he muttered to the dog. "Have a heart, Mac. You're making me look like a fool in front of a good-looking woman. If she had her glasses on she'd lose all faith in my manly proportions."

He could picture his rodeo buddies laughing themselves silly if they found out he'd spent Thanksgiving running around buck-naked, his genitals shriveling in the cold as he chased after a drunken dog. Remembering the rodeo gave Wyatt a sudden inspiration. He'd treat Mac like a balky calf and fake him out. Feinting left, Wyatt lured the dog to jump to the right. Then Wyatt leapt right, as well, and grabbed. He landed on the rug with enough force to knock the breath from him but at least he now had a grip on the Scottie.

"Did you catch him?" Charity asked.

"Yeah," he gasped. Struggling to his knees, he scooped the dog into his arms, glad for the animal's warmth against his bare chest. Carrying Mac into the bathroom, he shut the door. He deposited the Scottie on the floor and grabbed a towel to wrap around his waist. It didn't help much, but it was better than nothing. "Be a good dog," he said as he went back out the door.

He hurried to the kitchen for the broom. He didn't remember until he opened the pantry door that Charity had knocked the broom out the window a couple of hours earlier. He found a little whisk broom and a dustpan. That would have to do. As he started back to the living room he heard a steady crunching noise coming from outside the house.

Despite the cold, he walked closer to the back door and listened. Crunch, pause, crunch, pause. The sound was muffled, as if coming from . . . Wyatt snorted as he guessed what it was. Alistair was digging a tunnel between the two houses.

Something was seriously wrong with Nora's neighbor, Wyatt decided, checking the dead bolt on the back door before leaving the kitchen. If that loony got in the house, no telling what he'd do. Besides, Wyatt had no intention of being interrupted for the next few hours.

Returning to the living room, he glanced at the tousled beauty sitting on the window seat. She looked as if she'd lost her best friend, and he longed to toss aside the dustpan and concentrate on bringing a smile to those down-turned lips. And then a sigh. And a moan. His groin tightened.

"There you are," she said. "What took so long?"

"Miss me?"

"I—" She blushed, a very gratifying sight indeed. "Yes."

"Good. I missed you, too. But I controlled myself long enough to stop and listen to Updegraff trying to tunnel over here."

"You're kidding."

"Nope. I'm no expert on what tunneling through snow sounds like, but I'd bet money that's what he's doing. I checked the dead bolt on the back door." He walked to the front door and examined it, too, although he imagined it would take a very strong person to break through the snow packed around it.

"You think he wants to get *in?*" Charity's eyes widened and she wrapped the afghan tighter around herself. "Why would he want to get in here?"

"Why was he risking his neck running around on roofs trying to record our conversation?"

"I don't know."

Wyatt walked around the sofa. Approaching the first spray of shattered crystal, he crouched and started sweeping fragments into the dustpan. "I think he's some sort of sexual deviant who's picked up on the chemistry between us and wants to watch."

"Alistair? He's too dull to be perverted."

Wyatt glanced up. "Maybe not as dull as you think. You don't know what he gets in the mail in plain brown wrappers."

"I just don't believe he's sexually weird. Not Alistair."

"Then what is going on?" Wyatt moved to another spot and continued to sweep. "I can promise you he has more on his mind than a cup of sugar."

"Maybe he just wants to make a full report to Nora about how we've trashed her house. Wyatt, I need my glasses."

He paused in his sweeping. "You'd probably be better off if you couldn't see this."

She winced. "That bad?"

Rising to his feet, Wyatt assessed the one-hundred-and-twenty-year-old rug. The ivory background was now decorated with ink blots the color of a very fine merlot. "Not good," he said. "Maybe I should see if Nora has some of that foaming cleanser in the kitchen."

"No! The fabric might not hold up to some over-the-counter stuff. The only hope is taking it to a professional." Her shoulders slumped. "I'll just have Nora put the cleaning bill on my tab, along with the antique glasses, the back door, the balcony railing, the—"

"Turkey roaster!" Wyatt said. "That bird's burning. I can smell it."

"Wyatt, get me my glasses."

"In a minute. And don't try to get them yourself. I haven't swept up all the splinters." He put down the dustpan and grabbed the oven mitts.

"You're keeping me prisoner on this window seat on purpose!"

"I hadn't thought of that, but it's an idea." He grabbed the roaster from the fire and set it on the hearth. Smoke billowed into the room as he lifted the lid. He coughed and waved at the smoke with the oven mitt. A raucous buzzing filled the house as the battery-operated smoke alarm went off.

"How does it look?" Charity shouted above the sound of the alarm.

"Sort of two-toned."

"Meaning?"

The fire alarm stuttered into silence.

"It's sort of tan on the top and real black on the bottom," Wyatt said.

"You know what? I don't even care."

He grinned at her. "That's my girl. Ready to eat?"

She threw back the afghan and reached for her sweatshirt. "I'd chew on old shoe leather at this point."

The roaster lid dropped from his nerveless fingers and clattered to the hearth as he gazed upon paradise.

Her head jerked up. "Did you burn yourself?"

"No." He'd never seen anything more lovely than her rosy body framed by pristine snowdrifts just outside the window. Her burgundy nipples puckered in the chill and her full breasts quivered as she slipped her arms into the sleeves of the sweatshirt.

"Do you have to put that on?" he asked softly.

She paused. "It's cold, Wyatt."

Not from where he stood, it wasn't. "I'll build up the fire. We'll get more blankets to throw around us. In fact, let's drag the guest room mattress in here."

"You're suggesting we eat our Thanksgiving dinner naked?"

The towel around his waist twitched as the idea had a predictable effect on him. "Yep."

She pulled her arms out of the sweatshirt sleeves, tossed it aside and wrapped the afghan around her shoulders again. Then she winked at him. "Then you'd better build up that fire, cowboy."

The gleam in her eyes sent such heat rushing through him that he wondered if the fire would be overkill.

THANKSGIVING DINNER would never be quite the same, Charity decided as she sat on the edge of the mattress wrapped in a comforter. Now she'd always associate the holiday with a picture of Wyatt wrapped in a blanket as he carved the turkey. Even more enticing, the blanket kept sliding off his shoulders to reveal the play of muscles as he worked.

MacDougal lay in his basket, sleeping off his brief drinking bout. Charity had examined the little dog and decided he wasn't permanently damaged. Wyatt had poured out the rest of the wine and they'd decided not to open any more, just to be on the safe side.

"I want to be completely sober, anyway," Wyatt had said, his glance meaningful.

And so did she. At Wyatt's request she'd left her glasses off, which helped close her in an intimate circle with him. The sensation of cozy exclusion heightened as the light outside the window faded. With a sense of almost childish delight, Charity eliminated thoughts of anything or anyone beyond reach of the fire's glow.

11

"HOLD THESE and I'll get the rest of the stuff." Wyatt handed Charity two plates heaped with juicy chunks of meat.

She held the plates up to her nose and drew in a breath. "Smells heavenly."

He paused to enjoy the smile of anticipation on her face. Only consideration for her hunger kept him from forgetting dinner and pushing her back onto the inviting expanse of flowered sheets and comforters piled there for the night. Later. Charity's loving would provide the perfect dessert.

He reached for the bowl of homemade cranberry sauce they'd found chilling in the refrigerator. It was the famous Logan family recipe he remembered from when he was a kid, with bits of fruit remaining in the mix. He and Charity had agreed to let the cranberry sauce stand for tradition and had decided to finish out the meal with the cheese, crackers, apples and nuts Charity had brought in earlier.

"Did we remember to bring forks from the kitchen?" Charity asked, dishing herself some cranberry.

"No." Wyatt assessed the cutlery requirements of the meal. "Let's forget forks. We have plenty of napkins and I'm starving." He helped himself to cheese, crackers and a handful of nuts.

"Agreed." She filled her plate and paused. "But this is Thanksgiving dinner. Maybe we should take a minute to be thankful."

As he turned his attention to her, he had no trouble feeling thankful for the pleasure he'd received today. "You're right. That's what this holiday is supposed to be all about, isn't it?"

"So I hear. And I have a lot to be grateful for."

"So do I." He wondered if she counted his lovemaking on her list. That would be very nice. "And as for this snowstorm," he added, "we've had some problems, but all in all we've been very lucky."

"Yes, we have been."

"You're . . . good to have around in an emergency, Charity."

"Thanks. So are you."

He looked into her eyes and for the first time wondered how he'd manage his life when he could no longer look into those eyes. A particular woman's gaze had never been essential to him before. Perhaps circumstances were causing him to exaggerate the importance of this one. And perhaps not. He glanced away. "I think we've been properly thankful for the time being."

"Me, too." She sounded relieved that he'd ended the moment. "Let's eat."

ALISTAIR CHOSE his route carefully, coming up on the living room from the guest bedroom side of the house. He packed the walls of the tunnel with the snow he shoveled, creating an igloo effect that, along with his physical exertion, kept him reasonably warm. He'd brought a thermos of hot Earl Grey tea, and he sat down to enjoy the last of the brew.

His goal was the bay window. Not that he expected to see much through the icy windows, but he'd found a treasure in the bottom of a trunk that would come in *very* handy. Thank heavens, darling Cordelia had saved a few things from her career as a nurse.

As he rounded the front steps, he slowed his progress so his shovel wouldn't make as much noise. He didn't want to alert that sinister pair to his presence. His shoulders ached from the effort, but he couldn't stop now.

A long hour later he could tell from the shape of the foundation that he'd reached the bay window. Time to dig upward. Soon he could stand. Cautiously he brushed the snow away from the window until he reached solid ice. Then he unzipped a side pocket of his coat and pulled out dear, departed Cordelia's stethoscope.

WYATT DIPPED a chunk of turkey in the cranberry sauce and took a generous bite. "Mmm."

"Good, isn't it?"

He watched her lick cranberry from her fingers. "The best Thanksgiving dinner I've ever tasted."

"People always say that."

"But this time it's true. Admit it."

"It's been delicious." She reached for another cracker and the comforter slipped down her shoulder to give him a glimpse of her breast. She bit into the cracker and readjusted the comforter.

He leaned over and slipped the cover down again. "You're interfering with my Thanksgiving feast."

"Nonsense."

"Nope. The absolute truth. One of the reasons the meal tasted so good was that I knew you were sitting beside me with nothing on under that blanket. I never realized how much better food could taste when all your senses are aroused."

She glanced at him and there was a glow of sensuality in her eyes. "You're a naughty man."

"You've known that from the beginning. And you've taken shameless advantage of the fact."

"I've done no such thing!" She pulled the comforter tight around her again.

He smiled, knowing he'd pry it loose eventually. "Then why weren't you wearing any underwear earlier today?" He was getting a hankering for dessert. He put his plate on the hearth.

Pink tinged her cheeks. "I was in a rush."

"Oh, sure." He took her plate from her lap and set it down next to his.

Her chin lifted. "Come to think of it, why did you have condoms in your pocket after you'd told me we definitely wouldn't make love?"

"I forgot to take them out."

"Oh, *sure.*"

This morning he might have been intimidated by her combative tone, but he'd made love to her now, and he knew the passionate woman who lay beneath the belligerent surface. And he would not be deterred. He pried her fingers away from the comforter.

"Stop," she murmured, trying to hang on.

He held the back of her head and began a nibbling assault on her mouth while he fought persistently for control of her blanket. "Keep that up and you'll rip it. I'm sure it's an antique."

"I don't like the idea that you think I was trying to seduce you this morning. I wasn't."

"Does it matter now?" He managed to slide a hand beneath the comforter and capture her breast. Her heart was thudding in excitement, and he knew she would be his in another few moments. He took her lower lip between his teeth and raked softly. Then he looked into her smoldering eyes. "What's the matter? Afraid to make things too easy for me this time?"

"It's all been too easy for you. I've been too available, being stranded here. I couldn't get away."

"*We* couldn't get away," he corrected. He played with her nipple until it tightened beneath his fingers and her gaze grew smoky. "But there have been . . . compensations."

"Is that so?" A teasing, sensuous note had entered her voice. "You feel compensated for all your trouble, then?"

He cupped her breast more firmly and kneaded the soft flesh. "I not only feel compensated, I feel positively rich. Let go of the blanket, Charity."

Her eyes drifted closed and she arched into his caress. "What would Nora think if she walked in the door right now?"

"You know as well as I do that won't happen."

Her eyes snapped open. "Did you hear a scratching sound? From the window?"

"It's just the fire crackling." He'd heard the noise at the window, too, but in his present state he didn't much care if that idiot Updegraff was picking away at the ice on the window so he could get a peep show. The sofa hid them from view as long as they stayed down on the floor, anyway.

And he'd become impatient. He got a firm hold on the comforter and pulled. She let go all it once and he almost lost his balance. She laughed softly and stretched back on the sheets, her shoulders propped against a folded blanket. His breath caught at the sight of her lying there on the violet-sprinkled sheet. Firelight licked her soft skin, painting it with shades of copper and bronze.

"Vixen," he murmured.

"Devil," she countered, a saucy smile on her full lips.

He gazed down at her and fought to keep from immediately claiming what she offered. He needed a diversion so he could make this last a very long time. Glancing around, he was inspired by the bowl of cranberry sauce. He picked it up.

She looked uneasy. "What are you going to do with that?"

"Keep you guessing." He dipped his forefinger into the sauce.

"Wyatt—"

"Hold still or this will get on the sheets."

"You're going to make a mess. Don't." She grabbed his hand.

"Then I guess you'd better lick it off my finger before it drips on you."

"I don't want to lick it off your finger."

"Why not? It tastes good. Quick. A little piece of fruit is about to fall off." He set the bowl of sauce beside her and moved his finger closer to her mouth.

"How do you know I won't bite you?"

"That's the chance I'll have to take."

Holding his gaze, she brought his finger closer and her tongue flicked out to swipe at the piece of cranberry on the tip.

Even without watching her eyes darken, he would have known from the movement of her tongue when the sensuous nature of what he'd asked took hold of her imagination. She turned the task into a slow, lazy process, and after the cranberry sauce was gone from his finger, she pulled it into her mouth in a blatant gesture that made him throb with longing.

Then she released him. "How was that?" she asked in a voice throaty with passion.

"Very nice." He dipped his finger in again and painted a circle around each nipple. This time she made no protest about the mess. She was with him.

By the time he'd licked away all the sauce and bits of fruit, she was breathing hard. He painted her mouth with more sauce and plunged his tongue between her parted lips. She kissed him feverishly, and he grabbed the bowl beside her to keep it from tipping. They lapped at each other's mouths like puppies until she took hold of his face and pushed him slightly away.

"My turn," she whispered. "Give me the bowl."

He could barely talk. "Be careful," he choked out as he handed it to her.

"I'll be careful. You be still." She gave him a gentle shove to his back and rose to her knees beside him.

It wasn't an easy order to fill. As the cool cranberry dripped over his heated shaft he gritted his teeth to keep from gasping out loud. When she began cleaning the cranberry away with her tongue, he gave up all pretense of manly silence and groaned with pleasure. She took her time, and he nearly lost his mind.

"Charity...." He wasn't sure if he was speaking her name or begging for help.

She slid up beside him, her eyes heavy-lidded with passion, her voice sultry. "You called?"

"Give me the bowl. That's enough."

Her mouth curved in a seductive smile. "But there's more cranberry sauce left."

"Any more cranberry sauce and I'll go insane." He struggled to a sitting position. "Give me that thing."

"If you insist." She relinquished the bowl.

He leaned down and put it on the hearth next to their plates. Fortunately he'd slipped some condoms under one of the pillows they'd brought in from the guest bedroom. He was in no shape to get up and look for one.

He stretched out beside her and reached under the pillow. Nothing. Becoming more desperate by the second, he lifted the pillow and patted the sheet underneath.

"Looking for something?" she asked.

"Yeah. I'm sure I—" He paused as he figured out who had them. He glanced at her.

From behind her back she produced the packages, fanned out like a hand of cards. "Presto. I found your hiding place."

He reached for one and she held them behind her back again. "Let me do it."

He stilled. He'd never allowed any woman to do that for him, and he knew exactly why. He was afraid she wouldn't be thorough enough and somehow the darned thing would come off. And he would become a father. Once that happened, his carefree rodeo days would be over for good, because he'd never deliberately risk his life when a little kid might lose a daddy in the process.

He gazed deep into her eyes, searching for any sign of deceit. "Why?"

"Because."

It wasn't a reason, and he waited for paranoia to hit. When it didn't, he realized with astonishment that he wasn't afraid of Charity making a mistake with the condom. More earth-shattering still, he hoped she would. The realization that he wanted to make Charity pregnant stunned him.

Dazed by the significance of his new mind-set, he cupped her face and kissed her with more tenderness than raw passion. "Okay," he said. "Be quick."

She wasn't quick, and he soon understood that she was an amateur at this procedure. He liked the idea that she wasn't adept. He positively loved the way she fumbled earnestly at the task. He liked a lot of things about Charity—a lot of things that had very little to do with the act they were about to perform.

He was crazy to be inside her, but it was a different kind of urgency, a deeper need than the mere quenching of desire he'd craved before.

"There," she said in a breathless whisper.

"Come here," he said, guiding her over him, closing his eyes with the exquisite sensation when she enfolded him inside her. Then he looked up into her flushed face, with her golden hair wispy and tousled around her shoulders, and the most incredible thing happened. A lump of emotion closed his throat and he felt tears dampen his eyes. He blinked them away. Thank God, she was nearsighted. She probably hadn't noticed.

She braced her hands on either side of his head and leaned down to kiss him. He combed his hands through her hair and cradled her head as he answered that precious kiss with all the tenderness that filled his heart.

Her breath caught and she pulled her mouth slightly away from his.

He opened his eyes to look into hers. "What?" he murmured.

Confusion flickered in her gaze. "You seem . . . different."

And so he was, but the feeling was too new to speak aloud. He had to live with this feeling for a while, get used to what was a radical shift before he risked telling anyone. Especially the woman who had caused it, the woman who could bring him to his knees with a single word.

He cupped her cheek. "Of course I'm different. You're in charge this time. I'm not used to that."

The confusion cleared. "I'll just bet you aren't." She moved her hips provocatively. "Well, I'm in the saddle now, cowboy. And I'm staying on until the buzzer."

He guided her down for another kiss. "That's my fondest hope," he whispered. Then he abandoned himself to the glory of being loved by Charity.

ALISTAIR UNHOOKED the stethoscope from his ears and slid to a sitting position in the tunnel. Then he took off his stocking cap and wiped his damp forehead. Incredible. He felt as if he'd been listening to a rerun of Kathleen Turner and William Hurt in *Body Heat*. But he shouldn't be surprised, or even very shocked, he thought. Anyone who would plot to kill poor Nora was certainly depraved enough to do whatever they'd been doing with cranberry sauce.

Alistair would have liked to be able to see, but the tiny hole he'd scratched in the ice hadn't allowed him a view of anything. He wondered if the nephew had dressed up in the silk bathrobe again. Whips and chains were probably standard fare for these two. Nobody had ever taught them decent family values, that was for sure. Alistair was proud to say that he and Cordelia had never... Well, except for that one time... Cordelia had insisted on tying him to the bedposts with surgical tubing....

But that was only once, and not important to this investigation.

Alistair believed he had ample evidence now, even if he hadn't found the frozen entrails. The nephew had admitted to feeling fully compensated for his trouble. He'd even used the word *rich*. Then, in a particularly cruel exchange, Charity had wondered what Nora would think if she could see them in their sinful love nest. Of course the nephew had reminded her that wasn't about to happen. That should be enough for the police. It was certainly enough for Alistair.

Yet one thing troubled him. They'd made a vague reference to not being able to get away because of the storm. If the power came on, they might leave the house, empty Nora's accounts and head for Mexico before the police caught them. The power could come on anytime now.

Alistair faced the fact that he might be the only person who stood between these crazed killers and a clean getaway. He swallowed nervously at the thought of the upcoming confrontation. But he had one more ace up his sleeve—the old .357 Magnum he kept in the upstairs closet.

12

As she stared into the embers of the fire, Charity finally had to admit to herself she was lousy at this one-night stand business. Maybe it was just her, or maybe it was something lacking in the X chromosome that prevented women in general from enjoying a love 'em and leave 'em scenario.

Wyatt, sleeping quietly beside her, had been the perfect candidate to practice the technique on because he didn't want a permanent relationship any more than she did. And even though Charity didn't believe in marriage, she had sexual needs. Wyatt had certainly exposed that fact in graphic detail. The experiment had seemed like a good one, and in theory she should have been able to seduce Wyatt and walk away when morning came.

But morning was very nearly here, and she was no more ready to say goodbye than she was to set fire to her precious bookstore. But she'd let someone pull her fingernails out one by one before she'd ever admit that. Wyatt was probably just waiting for her to throw off her disguise as an independent woman and reveal herself as a husband-hungry spinster. Actually, she didn't care if Wyatt married her. She just wanted him to stay. Forever.

That was certainly a pipe dream. Even this delicious isolation they were enjoying couldn't possibly last much longer. The power might very well come on today and the roads would certainly be plowed soon. Once that happened and the cabs and trains were running, Wyatt needed to get back for his rodeo.

And that would be the end of that. She'd been a temporary amusement for him. He'd enjoyed himself, no doubt about that. He might even be willing to stop in again the next time he was in town. That should have been perfect for her. Instead it gave her the most painful heartache of her life.

A cold nose touched hers. She reached out and scratched behind MacDougal's ears. "Hi, Mac," she whispered. "Want to go out?"

The little dog whined softly.

She didn't doubt he needed a potty break. He'd been sleeping ever since he'd lapped up the wine last evening. She eased out from under the comforter and grabbed a nearby quilt to wrap herself in. She didn't bother looking for her glasses. She knew the hallway well enough to make it to the back door without them. Damn, but it was cold, colder than yesterday, she thought as she walked with the Scottie to the back of the house. After Mac took care of his business she'd better build up the fire again.

She had trouble getting the back door open and had to pull with all her might. Finally it gave. Mac started out, then whipped around and headed back inside. The cold took Charity's breath away.

"You have to go out there, Mac," she instructed the little dog. "Be quick."

He gave her a forlorn look and trotted out into the little tunnel Wyatt had made for him. Charity closed the door and stomped her feet to stay warm. In seconds Mac scratched at the door and she let him in.

"I hope you took care of everything. It's too cold for me to check." She locked the door, grabbed his bag of dry dog food and hurried back into the living room.

Wyatt was awake, a blanket around his shoulders as he stoked the fire. He glanced around. "Hi," he said softly.

"Hi, yourself." Charity's heart squeezed at the sight of his blurred image. She decided not to put her glasses on just yet. Glasses might bring everything into focus, and she'd rather live in a fuzzy dreamworld awhile longer. After pouring some food into Mac's bowl, she sat on the mattress and tucked her frozen feet under her while Wyatt finished feeding the fire.

He replaced the screen. Still crouched, he turned. "Think fast," he said, and launched himself at her, tumbling her backward onto the mattress.

Laughing, she wrestled with him as he tried to rub his beard-stubbled cheek against hers. "You'll be sorry if you give me whisker burns on my face," she warned breathlessly.

"Oh, yeah? How about down here?" He pinned her squirming body to the mattress and leaned down to stroke his cheek gently over her bare breast.

"You asked for it." She placed the sole of her foot on his thigh.

He yelped and released her. "What's that, a snowball?"

"My foot."

"Good Lord. Something must be done."

Before she realized what he planned, he'd burrowed under the covers to grab her ankles. Ignoring her protests and Mac's furious barking, he dragged her by her feet to the edge of the mattress and held her with her soles facing the fire. Then he began a vigorous massage of her feet.

She shoved the quilt away from her face and blew the hair away from her mouth. "Is this manhandling absolutely necessary?"

"Wouldn't want you to get frostbite. Or give it to me accidentally." He glanced over at the dog, who was watching with great interest. "Go lie down, Mac. This treatment may take a while."

The Scottie trotted over to his basket and flopped down.

"He's a pretty good dog when he's not drunk," Wyatt commented.

"I may not report that little incident to Nora."

"There's a lot I hope you don't report to Nora." His massage gentled, became more sensuous.

"And what will you give me to keep quiet?" she teased.

"This." His stroking now included the length of both calves.

"But my legs didn't get cold."

"Can't be too careful with these cases. Got to keep the circulation going." His attention moved to her knees.

Her circulation was improving by the second. By the time he reached her thighs, her circulation was positively tip-top.

He eased up beside her but kept one hand firmly between her thighs.

She sighed with pleasure as he probed deeper to tap her wellspring of desire. He stroked her lovingly and she arched into his touch. "Where . . . did an Arizona boy learn how to treat frostbite?" she murmured.

"Fact is, I don't know a thing about frostbite." Slowly he ended the caress and reached for a cellophane packet lying beside the mattress.

"You must." She reveled in his heated gaze as he sheathed himself. "My feet aren't cold anymore."

"Good." He moved over her. "Because I want you to put them around me. Wrap me up tight, Charity. Tight as you can."

She sensed a note of desperation in his request. For one wild, hopeful moment she wondered if perhaps he was as reluctant to end this rendezvous as she was. Then thought gave way to sensation as he set her world to spinning with the touch that only he possessed. She wanted this so much. Too much.

And if she imagined that his lovemaking was more intense, his cries of release stronger, she knew it could be her own longing that colored what they shared. Fighting tears, she held on very tight, just as he'd asked. When they both drifted off to sleep again, she still held him wrapped securely in her arms. Her last conscious thought was that he was holding her just as close.

A DEAFENING CRASH and scream from somewhere overhead jerked them awake. Wyatt leapt from the mattress and grabbed his jeans from a chair. As Mac headed for the stairs barking, Wyatt called him back.

Charity shivered as she stared up at the ceiling where everything was now spookily quiet. "What *was* that?"

"Don't know." After he pulled on his jeans, he ran to the window seat, scooped up Charity's sweat suit and tossed it at her before putting on the Syracuse sweatshirt. "But I'm betting Updegraff's involved."

"Wyatt, I need my glasses."

This time he didn't argue but snatched them from a table and handed them to her. "I'm going up there." He started off, Mac bounding at his heels.

"I'm right behind you." She pulled her sweatshirt over her head with trembling hands and put on her glasses. It looked as if she had no choice about facing reality now. By the time she started up the stairs Wyatt was already out of sight in the upstairs hall.

"Hold it right there!" screeched a voice. "Hold it or I'll shoot!"

Charity's step faltered and her heart pounded hard against her ribs. Alistair. And he had a gun.

"Take it easy, Updegraff," Wyatt said in a soothing tone, the kind someone might use for a wounded but dangerous animal. "You need some practice if you're gonna be an upper-story man, buddy. That's a hell of a hole you made in Nora's roof."

Cold whooshed down the stairway as Charity climbed to the landing and saw Wyatt, his hands in the air, standing outside Nora's bedroom. Mac stood beside him, his fur on end, a low growl coming from his throat.

"I am *not* your buddy," Alistair said. "And we all know that Nora won't be needing this roof anymore."

"We might not agree on that one, Updegraff. But I think one of us has been smoking those funny little cigarettes again, haven't we?"

"I have no idea what you're talking about."

Charity edged closer.

"That makes us even," Wyatt said. "Now, why don't you just put that pop-toy away and—"

"Never! I'm taking you in."

"In?"

"You're under arrest for the cold-blooded murder of Nora Logan, may God rest her soul."

Charity gasped.

"What?" Wyatt's mouth dropped open.

"You carelessly snuffed out the life of a fine woman, a good neighbor, a loyal friend, even if she never really appreciated that I—"

"I've had enough of this." Wyatt started forward.

"Stay there, I said!"

Wyatt backed up. In the process he motioned Charity away.

"Your partner in crime is out there, isn't she?" Alistair said, his tone hysterical. "She'd better get in here, too, if she doesn't want to see her lover shot."

Charity's throat went dry and she moved down the hall on wobbly legs. "I'm coming, Alistair. Don't get excited."

"Stay out of this, Charity," Wyatt ordered.

"Not on your life, cowboy."

"Contrary female. Get the hell back down the stairs. We've got a certified loony here who thinks we killed Nora."

"I don't *think* you did. I know it!" Alistair said. "I have all the proof I need to put you both in the slammer!"

Wyatt shook his head. "You're not only delusional, you sound like an old Jimmy Cagney movie. You need to update your routine, Updegraff."

"Go ahead, make fun of me. You've been doing it all along, both of you. But I'll have the last laugh. Truth will out."

"And just what makes you think we murdered Nora?" Wyatt asked.

"Motive and opportunity. And she's missing."

Charity edged down the hall. Wyatt was blocking most of her view through the door, but what she could see made her heart sink. Alistair sat in the middle of Nora's bed, or what used to be Nora's bed. The footboard had been destroyed by the huge oak branch that had apparently broken and crashed through the roof.

Alistair must have tried to use the tree to get onto the roof. A jagged hole the size of a compact car was open to the leaden sky, and nearly everything in the room was covered with snow. Had Alistair not happened to land on the bed, he might have been killed by the fall. And he did, indeed, have a very lethal-looking pistol pointed at Wyatt's heart. Cold sweat trickled down Charity's spine.

"Nora's not missing," Wyatt said. He sounded like the soul of patience, but a muscle twitched in his jaw. "She's still up in Maine, stranded by the same snowstorm that hit us."

"Up in Maine?" Alistair scoffed. "That cover story won't work with me anymore, Mr. I'll Inherit Everything. She checked out of her bed and breakfast three days ago."

"Maybe she found one she liked better."

"Likely story, Mr. Rodeo Star."

"Oh, for crying out loud, Updegraff. This isn't one of your mystery books. You've put two and two together and come up with seven squared. Let me—"

"I'm tired of playing around with you two." Alistair pointed the gun at Wyatt's forehead. "I see you lurking back there, Charity. Both of you get in this room before I have to start shooting."

"Dammit, Charity, leave. I can handle this better alone."

"That's what you think." She slipped under his up-raised arm and darted into the frigid room.

"Charity!" Wyatt roared.

She ignored him and concentrated on appealing to the persnickety nature of Nora's neighbor. For the time being she decided to go along with his belief that Nora was dead. "We have to clean up this mess, Alistair," she said. "The snow will devastate Nora's room. She would have been shocked to see this carnage. How can we preserve her memory if everything's ruined?"

"I didn't mean for this to happen," Alistair admitted. "I meant to climb onto the balcony and break in through the French doors. Then I was going to sneak down the stairs and catch you and the nephew *flagrante delicto,* so to speak."

"Lucky for you that didn't work," Wyatt said. "If you'd showed up while we were flagrante delicto, I would have had to *wringo* your little *necko,* so to speak."

Charity glanced around the room, looking for just the right distraction. She finally found it. "Oh, no, Alistair," she moaned. "That picture of Nora with her college roommates is covered in snow! As I'm sure you know, they signed the picture, and one is now a famous mystery author."

"I know. I have all her books."

"That photograph is irreplaceable. I'm sure she wanted you to have it."

"Really? She said that?"

"She certainly did. Just last week she mentioned that you would be the only one who would appreciate such a keepsake."

"She's right about that."

"But someone needs to clean the snow off before the signatures run."

Alistair looked worried. "All right. But no false moves."

Charity stepped over to the dresser. She picked up the picture in its heavy gilt frame and started brushing. "Thank goodness, the snow doesn't seem to have seeped inside," she babbled, not looking at Alistair, not wanting to telegraph her next move. As she whirled and threw the picture, she yelled at Wyatt to duck.

Wyatt hit the snowy floor as the picture frame connected with the side of Alistair's head and the gun went off with a roar. Then Wyatt jumped to a crouch and hurled himself at Alistair. The little man was too dazed to protest as Wyatt wrestled the gun away and hurled it through the hole in the roof.

"No! You should have kept it!" Charity cried.

"Why, do you know how to shoot?"

"No."

"That's what I figured, and I didn't want you playing with it and getting hurt while I'm busy putting a patch over that hole in the roof."

"Fine talk after I just saved your fanny!"

His chin jutted in defiance. "I'll have you know my fanny was perfectly safe!"

"Didn't look that way from where I stood, buster."

His jaw clenched. "Maybe you need your glasses adjusted."

"Maybe you need your attitude adjusted."

"Charity, so help me..." He glared down at her, but slowly the anger was replaced by the soft warmth of concern. "If something had happened to you..."

"I thought he was going to shoot you," she murmured, beginning to tremble again in the wake of the adrenaline rush that had sent her into the bedroom.

His expression grew tender. "Charity, I—"

"My head hurts," Alistair whined.

Wyatt glanced at him. "Let's hang him upside down in a snowbank."

"Good idea. Using snow, I mean. There's a nasty lump growing above his ear."

"Pardon me if I don't ooze sympathy for this nut."

"But we should put something on that lump to keep the swelling down."

"Be my guest. I'll keep an eye on him to make sure he doesn't try anything while you make a snowball."

Charity had no trouble coming up with enough snow. The floor was covered with it. She packed some in her hand, pulled a pillowcase from one of Nora's pillows and wrapped the snowball in it before applying it to Alistair's head. "Hold that," she instructed.

"Now you'll kill me, too," Alistair babbled as he sat in the middle of the collapsed bed holding the cold pack against his head. "You'll bury me in a shallow grave just like you did Nora. And cut out my entrails, just for sport."

Wyatt looked disgusted. "I'm beginning to see why folks decide to gag their captives."

"Please use a clean rag," Alistair begged. "And no duct tape."

Charity folded her arms. "What do you think we should do with him?"

Alistair looked from one to the other and shook. "Make it quick. Please, no torture. Nothing with cranberry sauce."

Wyatt and Charity gazed at each other.

Then Wyatt braced his hands on either side of Alistair and put his face very close to the little man's. "You seem to think I'm a dangerous character, so listen to this, and listen good. If you *ever* tell anybody what you heard here last night, I will personally feed your *cajones* to the sharks."

Alistair looked about ready to pass out. "Wh-what are *cajones?*"

"Use your imagination, buddy. And you have an impressive imagination, so that shouldn't be too hard for you."

Alistair gasped and placed his free hand over his crotch.

Wyatt's smile looked lethal. "Bingo." He pushed himself away from the bed and turned toward Charity. "We'd better get that hole repaired and do what we can for this bedroom."

"I don't think we can trust Alistair to run around loose while we clean everything up," Charity said.

"You're right. Let's take him downstairs. We'll use my rope."

"You're going to hang me, aren't you?"

Wyatt surveyed him with studied nonchalance. "Don't tempt me."

"Wyatt, stop. You're scaring him."

Wyatt glanced at her. "Seems only fair. After all, he scared the hell out of me."

"I thought you said your fanny was perfectly safe?"

"It was. It was your fanny that concerned me." He winked at her. "As always."

13

WYATT TIED Alistair to a dining room chair placed near the fireplace, built up the fire and left Mac to guard him. Then he and Charity pulled on jackets and boots before starting upstairs.

"How are you going to cover that hole?" she asked as they climbed. "We've burned almost all that scrap wood in the garage."

He decided she'd better know the worst of it. "I should tell you something about that scrap wood."

She paused, one hand on the banister. "Do I need to hear this right now?"

"Better now than after Nora gets home." He continued to climb. "But don't worry. I'll take the responsibility."

She followed him up the stairs. "I hate explanations that start like that."

"At the bottom of the pile was a diagram, explaining how to reassemble it."

"Into what?"

"An antique secretary. Apparently made for President Andrew Jackson in eighteen thirty-five."

"Oh, *Wyatt.*"

He glanced back at her. "I think old Andy would have approved of the decision to burn it, under the circumstances. Don't let it paralyze you. If we don't patch the roof soon, somehow, that sprinkler system in the bedroom ceiling will burst and the damage will be even worse.''

She cringed, then started resolutely up the stairs. ''I can't believe this. All I had to do was take care of Nora's house. That's all she wanted. Is it too much to ask of someone that they return your house in the same condition you left it?''

''Well, in this case—'' Wyatt stopped speaking to listen. Sure enough, there was a steady dripping sound coming from the direction of Nora's bedroom. He bolted down the hall and into the room with Charity right behind him. While they'd been downstairs with Updegraff, the sprinkler pipes had burst.

Wyatt stared at the soggy bed and ruined curtains. Even the wallpaper had begun to peel off, although that didn't matter much on the wall where Updegraff's .357 had blown a sizeable hole through the plaster.

''Perfect,'' Charity said. ''The only thing that could improve upon it would be a bomb.''

As if in response, a light flickered on beside her bed and the bulb shattered in the cold.

Wyatt gazed at her. ''Power's on.''

Charity met his gaze. ''Seems so.''

They weren't cut off from the outside world anymore, Wyatt realized. Help for this disaster was a phone call away. This might be his last chance to say what was on his mind. But without the cozy fire, the sense of intimacy, the sensuous mood they'd shared, words were difficult to come by. ''Charity, I—''

''Listen. Do you hear that?''

From outside came a distant sound of rumbling and scraping. Wyatt walked with Charity over to the French doors and they stepped out on the balcony. A snowplow was slicing through the drifts and sending snow spraying in rooster tails on either side of the blade. Right behind the plow was a slow-moving taxi.

Wyatt glanced down at Charity. "Nora?"

"I imagine so."

He took a deep breath. "Listen, before she gets here, I just want to say that—"

She placed a finger against his lips. Her blue eyes focused intently on his face. "Don't say anything, Wyatt. Just kiss me goodbye, the way we both planned all along."

The pain of her rejection nearly knocked him flat. So she had meant what she'd said about wanting her independence. She'd meant every blessed word. He wanted to cry out his devastation, but instead he pulled her to him in a fierce repudiation of her decision. He put everything he'd wanted to say into that kiss. And he imagined that she answered him with the urgent press of her body and the hunger of her mouth.

Yet she pulled away and stepped back. "Good luck in the arena, cowboy."

"Charity—"

"No. Don't trivialize this. I don't ever want to see you again." She turned and fled the room.

SATURDAY proved to be a very busy one for the bookstore. During the summer Nora had told Charity to hold on until Christmas before she gave up. Apparently the Christmas season had arrived full force in Old Saybrook, and the citizens of the town enjoyed buying books as gifts.

Charity saw Nora come into the store that afternoon and hoped customers would remain a buffer so she wouldn't have to face her mentor alone. She'd apolo-

gized for the disaster Friday morning before leaving in
the same taxi that had brought Nora home. Then she'd
sent a letter offering to pay for all the damages. She
doubted the letter had arrived yet, but apparently Nora
wanted to confront the issue in person.

Charity engaged several customers in lengthy conversations, trying to discourage Nora from hanging
around. Nora continued to browse the shelves as if she
had all day to wait.

Finally the last person left the store. Charity glanced
out the display window to see if anyone might be coming down the snowy walkway to rescue her from this
scene, but the flow of customers seemed to have
stopped.

Nora approached the cash register, a book of love
poems by Emily Dickinson in her hand. She carried
herself with the same regal poise as always, and her knit
suit and London Fog trench coat looked as smart as
ever. But, Charity thought, there was something different, something softer about her today. Maybe it was
the pink scarf tucked around her throat that gave her
cheeks such a rosy glow and made her gray eyes spar-
kle. Even her short gray hair seemed to wave more
gently around her face today.

"Hello, Charity," Nora said with a smile. "Business
looks good."

"It's been very good today." Charity put out her
hand for the book. It wasn't the sort of thing she'd expect Nora to buy for herself. "Would you like this gift
wrapped?"

"No, thank you. I want to write a special inscription
in it first."

"I see." Charity didn't see anything at all. She
couldn't imagine who Nora planned to give a gift of

love poems to. She concentrated on the cash register keys as she phrased her next question. "Did you receive my letter?"

"No. What letter was that?"

"I wrote to you and offered to pay for all the damages."

"Oh, that. Don't worry about the damage to the house, Charity. I'm well insured."

Charity glanced up, hot with shame. "Then maybe I could handle some of the chores of getting things back to rights. I'd be glad to take the rug to be—"

"I wouldn't hear of it. But there is something you could do for me."

"Anything, Nora. I feel terrible about the way things turned out."

"So do I."

A fresh wave of guilt washed over Charity. "I'm sure you do. That house was absolutely perfect, and—"

"Not about the house. That's totally unimportant. I'm talking about my nephew."

Charity's hand slammed down on the register and the drawer popped out with a clang. She closed it and became very busy refiguring the cost of Nora's book while she tried frantically to think of something noncommittal to say. She drew a complete blank. Worse yet, she was shaking uncontrollably.

"That man is miserable," Nora said. "I've never seen such a sad case."

"C-case?" Charity glanced up.

"Lovesickness."

Charity swallowed. Maybe she'd heard wrong.

"If you weren't interested in a commitment, why on earth did you lead that poor boy on?" Nora asked sharply.

Charity stared at her. "Lead him on? Wyatt Logan? Nobody leads that hardheaded cowboy anywhere!"

"You could, if you wanted to."

Charity clutched the edge of the counter. "You must be joking."

"I wouldn't joke about this, Charity. I love Wyatt with all my heart, and I hate to see him so unhappy. He's found himself in the sad position of wanting a woman who doesn't want him."

"That's not true!"

Nora lifted both eyebrows. "Really? Which part?"

"He...he doesn't want a woman to tie him down. He told me so more than once."

"Exactly when did he tell you that?"

"Right in the beginning. And then again on Thanksgiving morning. And—" Charity paused. She couldn't remember another instance, but there must have been one. Wyatt had been very clear. No ties. The message was burned into her aching heart.

"How about after the two of you made love?"

Heat rose into her cheeks and her throat closed in embarrassment. "He told you about that?" she murmured.

Nora chuckled. "He didn't exactly have to tell me, Charity, sweetheart. I mean, the rumpled mattress in front of the fire, the underwear on the window seat.... It didn't take a rocket scientist to figure things out."

Charity buried her hot face in her hands. "This is so embarrassing."

"I think it's time to tell you about my trip to Maine."

"Good idea." Charity brushed trembling fingers over her cheeks and cleared her throat. "How was your trip, Nora?"

"Fantastic. I spent most of it in bed with the most wonderful man."

Charity's mouth dropped open.

"That's why I wasn't in my appointed place when Alistair called to tattle on you two. I'd already moved into Stan's house. It was a great spot to wait out the storm."

"I had no idea," Charity whispered.

"You weren't supposed to have any idea. This was my secret, because I didn't know how it would turn out, and I didn't want anybody's pity if the whole thing fell flat." Nora picked up the book of love poems. "This book is for Stan. We're getting married next month."

There was a stool behind the counter, and Charity felt the sudden need to sit down. "Married?"

"Yes, and I'm inviting you, of course. Wyatt and his mother and dad will be there, so I thought you might want to work out this little problem so there'll be no awkwardness at my wedding."

Charity felt as if she'd just tumbled down *Alice in Wonderland*'s rabbit hole. "But you don't believe in marriage. You think it's a patriarchal trap!"

Nora looked uncomfortable.

Charity had never seen Nora look uncomfortable before. "Don't you?"

Nora fiddled with her scarf and readjusted the collar of her trench coat. Finally she met Charity's gaze. "It can be a trap. We've all seen that often enough. But—" She looked away again. "Oh, Charity, it's not easy admitting this after forty years of kidding myself. I still believe in all the feminist principles you grew up with, but I refused to admit there was anything good about marriage because...well, mainly because I didn't get the man I wanted. Turning my back on the whole institution was my defense against that heartbreak. I've been far too didactic, Charity. In the coming years I want to rectify that.''

Charity felt as if Nora had sucker-punched her in the stomach.

''Now, don't look like that,'' Nora scolded. ''I'm not about to dress up in cellophane or fetch my husband's slippers and pipe when he comes through the door each night. I think my marriage will be a better one than it would have been if I'd married forty years ago, because I'll demand an equal partnership and stand a chance of getting it. I don't look at this as a trap, Charity. It's an opportunity—for sharing, for communication.'' Her gaze softened. ''For love.''

The tension in Charity's stomach began to ease. Nora had always represented an unreachable ideal. Discovering Nora's human frailties lifted a burden Charity hadn't realized she carried until it began to slip away— the struggle to live up to what she'd perceived as perfection. ''This Stan must be quite a guy.''

''He is, and he was forty years ago.''

''The same man you couldn't have?''

She nodded. ''All because of my stubbornness. He was the star quarterback at Syracuse and I was the head cheerleader.'' She held up the football-shaped key ring. ''He gave me this forty years ago. And I've kept his college sweatshirt all this time.''

Charity remembered that sweatshirt well. The surprises just kept coming.

Nora smiled at her. ''Hard to believe I was a cheerleader, isn't it? But I was. Damned good at it, too. And crazy in love. Stan was drafted by the New York Jets about the time my parents died in the house fire. I became an heiress. I told Stan to forget his football career because he'd only end up getting hurt. We'd live on my money. He turned down my generous offer.''

"And forty years later he's changed his mind?"

"Not on your life. He made a pile of money in the NFL, invested well, and doesn't need a penny from me. The sad part is, we could have worked that out forty years ago.'' She looked directly into Charity's eyes. "Don't let the same thing happen to you and Wyatt.''

Charity gasped. "How did we get back to that?"

"We've always been talking about that. Haven't you been listening?''

"Of course! And your case is nothing like mine! Stan apparently wanted to marry you, he just didn't want to be controlled. . . .'' Charity stared at Nora.

"It's very easy, sweetheart,'' Nora said. "The two of you agree to love, honor, and respect the individuality of the other. You and Wyatt are smart people. I know you can do it.''

Charity's heart began to pound. "What makes you think he wants to try?''

Nora gave a hoot of laughter. "For the brief time he stayed on Friday, all he talked about was you. No intimate details, mind you. And you two must have put the fear of God in Alistair, because *he* won't even give me details, either. But, trust me, Wyatt thinks you hung the moon. I told him to go over to your house and tell you how he feels, but he's convinced you're a thoroughly modern woman who would throw a ring back in his face.''

"That's what I wanted him to think," Charity whispered.

"And would you?"

Tears brimmed in Charity's eyes. "No way.''

"As I thought." Nora shrugged out of her coat. "Show me how to work that cash register. I'm minding the bookstore for the weekend while you go to New York."

"Oh, Nora, I couldn't ask you to—"

"You didn't. I insisted. Look, I've been waiting to marry Stan for almost half a century." She rolled her eyes. "God, does that make me feel old. Anyway, I don't want a couple of hangdog faces lousing up the happiest day of my life." She pulled a piece of paper from her pocket. "Here's the phone number for Wyatt's hotel, but he'll probably be at the Garden by the time you arrive, so I'd go there first."

Charity took the paper in fingers icy with fear.

"Now get your coat on and get out of here." Nora waved her toward the back room. "You can still catch a train into the city if you move that little fanny of yours." She laughed. "Which was, I understand, the first part of you Wyatt fell in love with."

AFTER CHARITY LEFT the bookstore Nora picked up the phone and dialed her brother David in Arizona. "She's on her way to New York," she reported. "If that dim-wit son of yours has any sense, they'll be engaged by tonight."

"Have either of them mentioned the *L* word?" David asked.

"No, but they are both in deep. I *told* you this was the one for him, David."

"I hope you're right. This is the most catastrophe-filled matchmaking effort I've ever seen in my life."

"The snowstorm was an unexpected bonus. I wish I could take credit for it, but I can't."

"And the complete trashing of your house? You're delighted about that, too?"

"Who needs a house when you have love?"

David chuckled. "I never thought I'd hear those words come out of your mouth, sis. But I'm happy for you. And now we can finally show Wyatt the old scrapbooks of you in your cheerleading outfit."

"Don't get carried away, David. Listen, a customer is coming into Charity's bookstore. I have to go. I'll keep you posted."

"Do that."

Nora hung up the phone as Alistair pushed open the door, jangling the bell overhead.

He stopped short when he saw Nora behind the cash register. "What are you doing here?"

"I'm minding the store for Charity." She folded her hands on the counter. "What can I help you with, Alistair?"

Alistair pulled his scarf from around his neck. "I wanted to put in my order for the next Sue Grafton."

"And you planned to apologize to Charity, I expect."

Alistair looked surprised at the suggestion. "But it was an honest mistake. If they really had murdered you, you would have been happy to know that I acted so promptly in your behalf."

"If they really had murdered me, I wouldn't be happy or sad, Alistair. I'd be dead."

He waved a gloved hand. "Well, of course, technically, but speaking in the abstract sense, you certainly would have wanted someone to avenge the scurrilous—"

"Alistair, I appreciate your risking life and limb to avenge my imagined murder. However, you came perilously close to shooting two of my very favorite people in the process. In the future, please leave firearms out of your repertoire."

Alistair sniffed. "You needn't concern yourself about Alistair Updegraff's behavior any longer. You can house the entire Ringling Brothers Circus, complete with elephants, tigers and seals in your house and I won't lift a finger to interfere."

"Alistair, please don't think that I—"

"No, no." He waved a hand dismissively. "I understand that people don't appreciate neighborly gestures anymore. You don't have to hit Alistair Updegraff over the head."

"How is your head, by the way?"

"Better, thank you. But I'm through trying to go that extra mile. Times have changed."

Nora rested her chin on her hand and smiled at him. "If you say so. Want me to leave a note for Charity about the Sue Grafton book?"

"Uh, yes. And there, uh, was a book I ordered two weeks ago. It might be in, if you could check for me."

"Certainly. What is the title?"

Alistair shifted his weight and glanced up at the ceiling. "*Surveillance Techniques Made Simple,* I believe."

Nora waited until she got into the storeroom before she allowed herself a good laugh. In the midst of so much change, it was comforting to know that some things would always be the same.

14

CHARITY PAUSED before approaching the ticket window at Madison Square Garden. The crowd inside sounded like the ocean during a winter gale, and as Charity listened to the enthusiastic cheering she almost turned around. Wyatt was inside, perhaps the object of that cheering. With that kind of adulation, who needed a bookstore owner from Old Saybrook?

But she'd promised Nora she'd at least talk to him. Her promises to Nora were becoming increasingly difficult to keep.

She paid for her ticket and walked inside the circular building, where the roaring of the crowd drowned out any other sound. The sawdust-covered arena lay below her, bathed in lights and filled with the churning energy of the biggest bull she'd ever seen. A man flopped on the bull's back like a rag doll. He could be Wyatt or some stranger—Charity couldn't tell from this distance. It didn't matter. If the rag doll wasn't Wyatt at this moment, it would be soon. The thought made her stomach pitch.

The rag-doll man flew from the back of the whirling bull and landed in a crumpled heap in the sawdust. The crowd surged to its feet as the bull charged the downed cowboy. Rodeo clowns rolled barrels at the bull, distracting him, changing his focus.

Charity clutched her stomach and prayed she
wouldn't throw up. She couldn't do this. If Wyatt
needed to ride bulls to maintain his sense of self, she
wasn't the right woman for him, because she didn't have
the fortitude to hang around and watch. As it was, she'd
probably have nightmares for the rest of her life about
him being killed in the arena. She turned to leave.

"Charity!"

She swung back to find Wyatt Logan, rodeo cowboy, mounting the aisle steps toward her. Black leather
chaps encasing his legs rippled and spurs clanked as he
climbed upward. Light from the back of the auditorium winked off the polished championship belt buckle at his waist. His black Western shirt was unwrinkled,
his black Stetson dust-free. Obviously he hadn't been
the cowboy thrown just now. She fought the urge to run
into his arms. That wouldn't help her do the right thing,
which was to leave this man to his dangerous life-style.

"How did you know I was here?" she asked.

"Nora had me tracked down." He reached her and
paused about two feet away.

Charity breathed in the scent of animals, sweat and
dust. She'd never experienced such a powerful aphro-
disiac.

"Nora said to expect you about now," he said, "so
I've been watching. I saw you come in." He adjusted his
black hat. "Looked as if you were about to leave."

She relearned the rugged planes of his face, the
sculpted beauty of his mouth, the comforting breadth
of his shoulders. She wanted him so much, but she
couldn't be the kind of woman he needed. "I shouldn't
have come."

"Why did you?"

"Because Nora said...because I thought...never mind. I should have left it the way it was. I'm sorry, Wyatt." Drawing on strength she didn't know she had, she turned and started toward the door.

"Wait." He grabbed her arm and pulled her around to face him.

She noticed they'd attracted the attention of people sitting in the back of the auditorium. They craned their necks to get a better look at what was obviously one of the rodeo stars. "We have an audience," she murmured, gazing up at him.

"I'm getting used to that." A muscle worked in his jaw and he kept his hand clamped firmly on her arm. "Something made you show up here tonight. I want to know what it was."

"Well..." Even through the quilting of her jacket she could feel the strong print of his fingers. She looked into his face, shadowed by the broad brim of his hat. His stern expression, combined with boots and a hat that made him seem taller and more imposing, intimidated her. She had a hard time squaring this image with the man who had lived with her so intimately. "I guess you know Nora's getting married," she said.

"I do."

"It's probably just the romantic fog she's in that made her talk like this, but she seems to think that you and I shouldn't...reject the idea out of hand. But, of course, I know how you feel, so—"

"Don't bet on it."

Her heart skipped into a higher gear as she gazed into his eyes.

There was no softening of his expression, no hint of a smile. "If a guy's going to survive on the rodeo circuit he has to learn to adjust. He may have a technique that's worked great for years, and then he hits the moment when it doesn't work anymore. If he can't adjust, can't innovate, he'll be gone.''

She could barely breathe. "And you...hit that moment?''

"About three o'clock Thursday afternoon.''

When they'd first made love. She began to tremble.

"But when I tried to talk to you about it, you cut me off. I figured I was the only one who'd changed and I'd have to find a way to live with it. Then you showed up tonight. And you still haven't told me why.''

"Because I changed my mind, too.''

The fierce light that leapt into his eyes broke her heart because she knew her next words would extinguish it.

"But it won't work, Wyatt.''

The light blazed higher in his eyes. He captured her other arm in the same iron grip and pulled her close. "That's so typical of you, Charity Webster. You're the queen of obstacles, but I'm not letting you get away with it this time. All I need to know is that you want me. The rest is details.''

"Big details,'' she protested, beginning to panic.

"Well, here's the biggest one of all. I love you, you contrary woman.''

Her whole world erupted in fireworks. "Oh, Wyatt.''

He gave her a little shake. "*Oh, Wyatt?* Is that the best you can do?''

She forced out the words. "What difference does it make if I love you? We can't get married!''

"Trust me, it makes a huge difference. Say it.''

"I love you, but—''

"Without the *but.*''

"I love you!''

"Finally." He swept off his hat and kissed her with such competence that her glasses steamed up and she forgot the rows of people sitting a few feet away. She forgot the rodeo. She forgot the reason why she couldn't marry this incredibly sexy cowboy.

Then he released her. "Gotta go. I'm up in fifteen minutes."

"But that's exactly—"

"No time, Charity." He backed away from her and put on his hat. "We'll talk when I'm finished. We'll work out those details that've put a twist in your knickers."

"I don't want to watch!"

He pulled the brim of his hat low over his eyes. "So take off your glasses. Just don't leave."

"I suppose you think just because I love you that you can order me around!"

He grinned at her. "*Please* don't leave, then. I need you here." He turned and took the steps down to the arena two at a time.

Charity watched him until he disappeared in the crowd of cowboys surrounding the bucking chutes. When she became aware that several people had swiveled in their seats to gaze at her with bemused smiles on their faces, she realized she'd just shouted out her declaration of love loud enough for people several rows down to hear.

"Well, how would you like it if the man you loved was about to climb on one of those brutes?" she questioned the group in general.

An attractive redhead sitting on the aisle laughed. "Honey, if you don't like it, go get yourself an accountant and pass that gorgeous cowboy on to me."

Then the bull and rider scheduled just ahead of Wyatt broke from the chute and everyone returned their attention to the arena. Charity forced herself to watch, too. The sight of the twisting, heaving bull still made her mouth go dry and her pulse race, but she was calmer than she'd been the first time around. However this cowboy wasn't Wyatt.

He was thrown off, but he got up immediately, ran for the fence and climbed over before the bull got to him. Then the announcer introduced Wyatt Logan as the next rider up and listed his many accomplishments. The crowd cheered.

Charity remained standing, but knew she'd couldn't run away, not after Wyatt had said he needed her. Somehow she'd would watch him ride this bull and pray he survived the experience. Then she'd explain her position—she couldn't ask him to give up bull riding, so she'd be on her way.

It was the longest eight seconds of her life. She didn't take off her glasses, didn't close her eyes, didn't blink, didn't even breathe, as if only total concentration would protect him from harm. Her enemy, the creature who could blot out all that was important to her, was a brindle monster, bigger than either of the two bulls she'd seen before. He leapt, whirled, twisted and lunged, the bell around his neck clanging a furious warning.

Sweat trickled down her back and her palms stung from the bite of her nails. The black figure on the bull's back jerked spasmodically each time the animal crashed back to earth, but bull and rider stayed connected. After an eternity of pain the buzzer sounded, and Charity jumped as if awakened from a trance. The bull charged past a fence and Wyatt jumped. Hands grabbed at him, hauling him over the fence into safety. Charity's knees wobbled. She staggered to the first step going down the aisle and sank down, breathing hard.

WYATT ACCEPTED congratulations from his friends while trying not to seem impatient. At last he was able to excuse himself, circle the arena and start back up the aisle toward Charity. He'd banged his leg on the fence as he went over and he tried not to limp as he climbed the stairs. Charity would probably give him hell for hurting himself.

She sat on the steps high above him, and a light on the back wall shone down on her golden hair, creating a halo. Wyatt chuckled. Much as he loved this woman, he knew she was no angel. He wouldn't have wanted one of those, anyway. This opinionated, feisty, courageous female was the only one for him. For once Aunt Nora had been absolutely right.

As he approached, he couldn't keep the grin off his face. He'd just ridden the toughest bull on the circuit to the buzzer, and he was going to marry the sexiest woman in the world. Life was good. Of course, Charity wore an expression of doom, but he'd fix that.

He mounted the last step, turned and winced as he sat down beside her.

"You're hurt."

"It's nothing. I rode him, Charity."

She glared down at her feet and wouldn't look at him. "I know."

"You watched?"

"Yes, and I won't ever do it again. I can't ask you to give up bull riding, so that's it. We have no future."

He'd pretty much expected this, but he could deal with it. "Why can't you ask me?"

She lifted her head and stared at him. "Because the whole idea is for each of us to be whatever we want to be. I can't ask you to be somebody different."

He reached for her left hand and placed a kiss on her ring finger. "What I want to be is your husband."

She made a funny little choking sound before clearing her throat. "You—you mean, you'd give up bull riding for me?"

He gazed at her. He'd give up breathing if she asked him to, but he decided against broadcasting just how far gone he was. "Sure."

"But wouldn't you resent that?"

"Not if we could work out a compromise." He turned her palm up and placed a kiss there. He was gratified at the slight tremor that ran through her hand at the contact. "What would you say if I switched to saddle broncs for the time being?"

As he'd expected when he'd planned this, she looked relieved. "Saddle bronc riding does sound better. At least there's that saddle for you to hold on to, and a horse sounds like a far easier animal to manage than one of those bulls."

"It does, doesn't it?"

"Uh, what did you mean, for the time being?"

"Until we have a baby. Then I'll quit for good."

"A baby?" Her eyes filled with such warmth that he cursed himself for not taking her off to some secluded corner for this discussion.

"That'll be your compromise, having the baby, since you didn't seem too excited about having children."

She reached a hand to his cheek. "I didn't really mean that. I want to have your baby," she murmured.

Desire surged through him. He took both her hands and stood, pulling her to her feet. "Let's get out of here.

They can mail me my buckle.'' He pulled her down the steps. ''We'll get my stuff, and I'll introduce you to my buddies. They can pick up my prize money.''

''I don't think you should just leave like this, Wyatt.''

''Don't think just because I love you that you can tell me what to do, Charity.''

Fortunately she laughed. ''Okay. It's your rodeo.''

He paused. ''So, do we have a deal? I'll switch to saddle bronc riding and you'll get pregnant?''

Her mouth curved in that saucy smile that drove him wild. ''I'll do my part if you'll do yours.''

''Oh, I'll do my part.'' He pulled her into his arms for a quick kiss. ''Often and well,'' he murmured as the glow of sensuality filled her eyes.

He'd have to get her through the introductions to his friends in a hurry, he thought. Not only was he eager to get back to the hotel, he didn't want her talking to the guys and asking questions. Knowing Charity's quick mind, it wouldn't take long before she discovered that he'd tricked her just a little. He wanted her to be completely bound to him before she learned what every rodeo cowboy worth his spurs knew—saddle bronc riding was the most dangerous event of all.

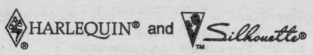

HARLEQUIN® and Silhouette®

are proud to present...

HERE COME THE GROOMS™

Four marriage-minded stories written by top Harlequin and Silhouette authors!

Next month, you'll find:

The Bridal Price	by Barbara Boswell
Annie in the Morning	by Curtiss Ann Matlock
September Morning	by Diana Palmer
Outback Nights	by Emilie Richards

ADDED BONUS! In every edition of *Here Come the Grooms* you'll find $5.00 worth of coupons good for Harlequin and Silhouette products.

On sale at your favorite Harlequin and Silhouette retail outlet.

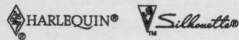 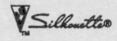

You are cordially invited to a
HOMETOWN REUNION

September 1996—August 1997

Bad boys, cowboys, feuding families, arson,
babies, mistaken identity, a mom on the run...
Where can you find romance and adventure?
Tyler, Wisconsin, that's where!

So join us in this not-so-sleepy little town and
experience the love, the laughter and the
tears of those who call it home.

WELCOME TO A
HOMETOWN REUNION

They're still talking about the last stranger
who came to Tyler, and now there's another.
He's an arson investigator with a job to do.
But...his prime suspect's daughter and her
kids make it increasingly hard for him
to do what he must.

The Reluctant Daddy by Helen Conrad

Available in October 1996
at your favorite retail outlet.

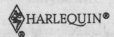

Look us up on-line at: http://www.romance.net

HTR2

The collection of the year!
NEW YORK TIMES BESTSELLING AUTHORS

Linda Lael Miller
Wild About Harry

Janet Dailey
Sweet Promise

Elizabeth Lowell
Reckless Love

Penny Jordan
Love's Choices

and featuring
Nora Roberts
The Calhoun Women

This special trade-size edition features four of the wildly popular titles in the Calhoun miniseries together in one volume—a true collector's item!

Pick up these great authors and a chance to win a weekend for two in New York City at the Marriott Marquis Hotel on Broadway! We'll pay for your flight, your hotel—even a Broadway show!

Available in December at your favorite retail outlet.

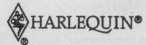 

REBECCA

43 LIGHT STREET

YORK

FACE TO FACE

*Bestselling author Rebecca York returns to "43 Light Street"
for an original story of past secrets, deadly deceptions—and
the most intimate betrayal.*

She woke in a hospital—with amnesia…and with child.
According to her rescuer, whose striking face is the last
image she remembers, she's Justine Hollingsworth. But
nothing about her life seems to fit, except for the baby
inside her and Mike Lancer's arms around her. Consumed
by forbidden passion and racked by nameless fear, she
must discover if she is Justine…or the victim of some mind
game. Her life—and her unborn child's—depends on it….

Don't miss *Face To Face*—Available in October, wherever
Harlequin books are sold.

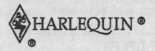

HARLEQUIN ®
®

As Seen on TV!

Free Gift Offer

With a Free Gift proof-of-purchase
from any Harlequin® book, you can receive
a beautiful cubic zirconia pendant.

This stunning marquise-shaped stone is a genuine cubic
zirconia—accented by an 18" gold tone necklace.
(Approximate retail value $19.95)

Send for yours today...
compliments of ◆HARLEQUIN®

To receive your free gift, a cubic zirconia pendant, send us one original proof-of-purchase, photocopies not accepted, from the back of any Harlequin Romance®, Harlequin Presents®, Harlequin Temptation®, Harlequin Superromance®, Harlequin Intrigue®, Harlequin American Romance®, or Harlequin Historicals® title available in August, September or October at your favorite retail outlet, together with the Free Gift Certificate, plus a check or money order for $1.65 u.s./$2.15 can. (do not send cash) to cover postage and handling, payable to Harlequin Free Gift Offer. We will send you the specified gift. Allow 6 to 8 weeks for delivery. Offer good until October 31, 1996 or while quantities last. Offer valid in the U.S. and Canada only.

Free Gift Certificate

Name: _____

Address: _____

City: _____ State/Province: _____ Zip/Postal Code: _____

Mail this certificate, one proof-of-purchase and a check or money order for postage and handling to: HARLEQUIN FREE GIFT OFFER 1996. In the U.S.: 3010 Walden Avenue, P.O. Box 9071, Buffalo NY 14269-9057. In Canada: P.O. Box 604, Fort Erie, Ontario L2Z 5X3.

FREE GIFT OFFER   084-KMF

ONE PROOF-OF-PURCHASE

To collect your fabulous FREE GIFT, a cubic zirconia pendant, you must include this original proof-of-purchase for each gift with the properly completed Free Gift Certificate.

084-KMF

Merry Christmas, Baby!

A romantic collection filled with the magic
of Christmas and the joy of children.

SUSAN WIGGS, Karen Young and
Bobby Hutchinson bring you Christmas wishes,
weddings and romance, in a charming
trio of stories that will warm up your
holiday season.

MERRY CHRISTMAS, BABY! also contains
Harlequin's special gift to you—a set of
FREE GIFT TAGS included in every book.

Brighten up your holiday season with
MERRY CHRISTMAS, BABY!

Available in November at
your favorite retail store.

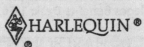

MCB

You're About to Become a *Privileged Woman*

Reap the rewards of fabulous free gifts and benefits with proofs-of-purchase from Harlequin and Silhouette books

Pages & Privileges™

It's our way of thanking you for buying our books at your favorite retail stores.

Pages & Privileges™

**Harlequin and Silhouette—
the most privileged readers in the world!**

For more information about Harlequin and Silhouette's PAGES & PRIVILEGES program call the Pages & Privileges Benefits Desk: 1-503-794-2499

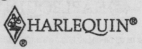

HARLEQUIN®

LL-PP18